W9-AAP-072

MISTLETOE AT MOONGLOW

A Christmas Novella

Deborah Garner

Cranberry Cove Press

Mistletoe at Moonglow
by Deborah Garner

Copyright © 2015 Deborah Garner
ALL RIGHTS RESERVED

First Printing – November 2015
ISBN: 978-0-9960449-4-3

This is a work of fiction. Names, characters, places and incidents either are products of the author's imagination or used fictitiously. Any resemblance to actual events or locales or persons, living or dead, is entirely coincidental.

EXCEPT FOR BRIEF TEXT QUOTED AND APPROPRIATELY CITED IN OTHER WORKS, NO PART OF THIS BOOK MAY BE REPRODUCED IN ANY FORM, BY PHOTOCOPYING OR BY ELECTRONIC OR MECHANICAL MEANS, INCLUDING INFORMATION STORAGE OR RETRIEVAL SYSTEMS, WITHOUT PERMISSION IN WRITING FROM THE COPYRIGHT OWNER/AUTHOR.

Printed in the U.S.A.

Also by Deborah Garner

Above the Bridge
The Moonglow Café
Three Silver Doves
Cranberry Bluff

For my mother,
who always made holidays special for us.

CHAPTER ONE

A whisper of snowflakes brushed against Mist's face as she stood in the doorway of the Timberton Hotel. It was a night like many other winter nights, the brisk air invigorating, a thin layer of snow coating the empty street, soft under the dim lights. The magical feeling of these evening reflections always warmed her heart. It was as if a Christmas card had come to life and she'd stepped into a peaceful scene that had been only paper a moment before.

Behind her, the glow of the hotel's fireplace mixed with the aroma of nuts cooking in a cinnamon glaze. Although it was Mist's first Christmas at the hotel, she knew Betty made cinnamon glazed walnuts every holiday season to keep in a bowl in the parlor. Townsfolk were reputed to stop by frequently, resulting in a slightly lower number of nuts in the candy dish each time.

That was just how Betty was, always doing something to please others. She treated everyone like family, always welcoming them into the hotel for a cup of fresh-brewed coffee or a slice of apple strudel. If not for Betty's generosity, Mist might have been homeless after losing her business, Moonglow Café. Or she might have returned to California, where she lived before arriving in the small town of Timberton, Montana. Instead, Betty had offered her a place to stay, as well as work. And it made sense. The hotel needed her and she needed the hotel.

Mist closed the door, not wanting to let in too much of the cold night. It would be a quiet evening, the last until after the holidays. Since guests wouldn't arrive until the next day, Mist had a chance to put the final decorating touches around the hotel's common rooms, as well as to deliver a surprise of some sort to each guest room. This was one of the benefits of living and working in the hotel. Betty had given her free reign to use her artistic talent to spruce up the lodging any way she desired. One whim at a time, Mist surprised guests and townsfolk alike with floral arrangements, unexpected trays of culinary treats, or her favorite: miniature paintings.

Art had been Mist's first passion, long before her love for cuisine took flight. She still thought fondly of evenings in front of her easel, the Pacific Ocean's surf in the background, the glow of the moon across its surface. Those enchanted times, after hours working on the deck of an ocean side restaurant, had formed the bridge between her love of painting and her love of cooking. She would blend mustard and grape seed oil during the afternoon and mustard-hued oil paint at night, satisfied at the end of the day with the balance the two art forms created in her life.

"Mist, dear, are you out there?"

Mist followed the voice, moving into the kitchen, where she found Betty sliding a spatula between a sheet of wax paper and several rows of glazed nuts.

"These are cool enough now. Let's refill the dish on the registration counter again."

Mist smiled. "You know those neighborhood boys are just tiptoeing in to swipe them when you aren't looking."

"Of course I know that," Betty laughed. "And why shouldn't they? Everyone needs a treat now and then." She set the spatula down and ran her hands over her apron, an old-fashioned style with a mixed print of holly and candy canes.

"*You* are a treat, Betty." Mist touched the hotelkeeper's shoulder before retrieving the crystal bowl from the front hall. Returning to the kitchen, she filled the dish to the brim, the crystallized glaze catching the light from the overhead lamps.

"That she is!" Both women looked up to see Betty's beau in the doorway.

"Now, Clive, you hush up," Betty chirped. "What brings you out on this snowy night, anyway?"

"I'd say the rumbling sensation in my stomach has something to do with it. Though it's always nice to run into a couple of pretty girls." Clive reached around Betty and grabbed a walnut before she could swat his hand away from the glazed nuts. Clive sat on a kitchen stool.

Mist watched the two senior lovebirds and smiled. The hotelkeeper and gem gallery owner had only recently admitted their feelings for each other after decades of misunderstanding. This was just one of many small miracles Mist had witnessed since arriving in Timberton a few months before.

"I'll whip something up for you," Mist said, heading for the refrigerator.

"I don't think there's such a thing as you just 'whipping something up,'" Clive said. "What you do with food is pure magic."

"Isn't that the truth," Betty added. "Speaking of which, you should see what Mist has planned for Christmas meals this year. Our guests have no idea what's in store. They're used to my turkey, mashed potatoes and dinner rolls."

"Which has always been a fine meal," Clive said.

"That's kind of you to say, Clive." Betty rolled another glazed walnut in Clive's direction, to thank him for the compliment.

"There's nothing wrong with a great, basic meal," Mist said. "Especially when it's served with affection and kindness, the way you do. I've heard the townsfolk talk about it. They always love coming to the Timberton Hotel for their holiday meals."

"Well, now they love coming to *every* meal," Betty said. "Having you set up Moonglow in the front parlor is one of the best things that has ever happened to this hotel, Mist. The guests love it, and the whole town appreciates the luxury of fine dining right here in Timberton."

"And they *really* appreciate not having to go to Wild Bill's." Clive couldn't help but laugh at his own comment.

"Now, Clive, you know William Guthrie still gets his regular morning crowd," Betty said. "Some people just need their greasy eggs and burnt toast. It's their habit."

"You're not about to break into the *Cheers* theme song, are you?" Clive rubbed his hands together as Mist set a plate in front of him. He looked at the meal and then looked up.

"How do you do this? Pull something together this fast? You didn't even know I was coming over."

Betty and Mist exchanged looks.

"OK," Clive admitted. "So you knew I'd show up when I got hungry enough. But, still."

"We had the main course in the oven on 'warm' and the rest in the refrigerator. Clayton and the guys from the fire department came over for dinner. Besides, Betty and I have to eat, too, you know." Mist turned away, as if serving boeuf bourguignon and chilled pear halves with a cranberry-pecan garnish was an everyday occurrence. In fact, it was exactly what could be expected at Moonglow.

"Well, I thank you," Clive said. "We're certainly spoiled."

"Good that you know it, Clive," Betty said.

Mist sat at the table, a mug of green tea in one hand, the hotel's registration book in the other. She set the mug down and browsed through upcoming reservations. "We have three check-ins tomorrow."

"Yes, all return guests." Betty covered a bowl of extra walnuts with plastic wrap and set it aside. "Clara Winslow will be here for the first time without her husband, who passed away this year."

"This will be a difficult time for her," Mist said. "We'll try to make it special somehow, in spite of her loss. What about Michael Blanton?"

"Very quiet man, mid-thirties, I'd say. He'll sit by the fire and read most of the time. He's been coming here for the holidays for a good ten years."

"And the Morrisons? The notes show they're a party of three."

"Yes, they'll have a child with them, a boy," Betty said. "Our only guests with children this year. Nice family. Stayed here two years ago, but missed last year."

Mist turned the page to the list of arrivals for the following day. Her earrings, dangling trails of beads and feathers, swayed as her head moved. "Just two arrivals the next day."

"That's right," Betty said. "It'll be a small crowd this year, but an interesting one. Neither guest coming in that day has been here before. I believe one is a professor from England who's a visiting lecturer up at the University of Montana. He'd planned to go back to London for the Christmas break, but time and airfares made it unreasonable. The other is a woman from Arizona. I don't know anything about her, though she originally made a reservation for two, and she changed it to one. I do know she's never seen snow before. She sounded excited about that."

"This is great," Clive said, the first time he'd spoken since the discussion about incoming guests started.

"Yes, wonderful," Mist agreed. "Such interesting people coming together for the holidays, some knowing nothing about the others, some meeting up again."

"He means the food," Betty laughed. "He wouldn't be getting sentimental about people meeting for the holidays."

"Not true," Clive protested. "I'm plenty sentimental about spending the holidays with you two lovely ladies. But I confess, I was talking about Mist's cooking."

"See? I told you." Betty looked pleased with herself. "We'll have to watch out during the cookie exchange, to make sure he doesn't hover too close and gobble up the goods."

"That's right," Clive said. "That's tomorrow, isn't it? When you women folk gather here to trade cookies and gossip?"

"It's not restricted to women, Clive," Betty corrected. "Anyone in Timberton is welcome to bring a plate of cookies to exchange. We can't help it if you men don't participate."

"But we do!" Clive protested. "I participate every single year."

"Exactly how do you figure that?" Betty laughed, already knowing what his answer would be.

"Well, now," Clive said, "I consider taste testing to be serious business. And you know you can depend on me for that. You might think of me as your quality control specialist."

"I'll admit you're onto something there, Clive." Betty grinned. "No use baking cookies every year without someone to confirm the cookies meet our long-established standards."

"There you go." Clive nodded, satisfied he'd made his point. "But I do know I'm a little spoiled when it comes to food around here. So, thank you."

"You're very welcome, Clive," Mist said. "It's a pleasure to prepare food for you. I always know you'll eat every last bite."

"I'm surprised he doesn't lick the plate." Betty laughed as she crumpled a wax paper sheet and tossed it in the trash.

While her back was turned, Clive mimed licking his plate. Mist smiled and shook her head, beads and feathers swaying again.

"So we'll have seven hotel guests for Christmas Eve dinner and Christmas brunch," Mist clarified. "And how many from the town?"

"You can count on another thousand from here," Clive said, barely suppressing a grin.

"Clive, stop that. Don't scare the girl on her first Christmas here," Betty scolded. "You know Timberton doesn't have that kind of population, especially in the winter. There can't be more than fifty people in town right now, and some of them will leave to visit family."

"I'm figuring thirty total, plus hotel guests," Mist said. "Based on what people have told me over the last couple weeks."

"You might count on a few more," Betty cautioned. "We've had some calls from out of the immediate area. The word is getting around about Moonglow."

"She's right, Mist," Clive agreed. "You've put Timberton on the map."

"I'll make sure there'll be enough food to go around, don't worry." Mist stood, straightening her dark blue rayon skirt, which fell mid-calf, just above her work boots.

"What's on the menu?" Clive pushed his empty plate away and rubbed his stomach, as if ready to eat his Christmas meals right then.

"You'll just have to wait and see, Clive." Mist paused in the kitchen doorway. "You know there are always surprises in store at Moonglow." Smiling, she slipped out the door.

CHAPTER TWO

Mist lit the kerosene lantern and placed it on the table next to her bed. Though a flip of a switch would have let the marvels of modern electricity light the room, the softer glow of the lantern always fit her evening mood.

Sketchpad in her lap, she curled up on the bed and stared at the blank page, envisioning the scenes that would unfold over the next few days as the guests arrived. A widow, revisiting a favorite lodging, without the husband who'd always been with her. A child, the only one in a hotel full of adults. Two single men, both scholarly, she imagined, based on one's profession and the other's reading habits. And a woman from Arizona, who had never seen snow. Each person would bring varied energy to the mix.

Of course, there were the townspeople, as well. She had already expected a larger crowd than Betty and Clive predicted. There weren't any other options for dining, other than staying home. And a few might do that. But more would show up, not just to be fed, but for the camaraderie. Clayton, the fire chief, and his crew, were always guaranteed to be there. The same was true of Marge, who ran the local candy shop, plus a few other regular Timberton folks.

And then there was Hollister, the town's one homeless person. Mist had kept watch over him since she first arrived in Timberton. He might not sit at a table with others, his reaction to social situations still unpredictable. But she knew he would eat whatever she fixed for him, just as she knew he would be grateful.

She picked up a charcoal pencil, closed her eyes and opened them again, transferring the images of Christmas Eve dinner and Christmas brunch from her imagination to paper. She could see it clearly when she planned a meal – not just the menu or food, but the table setting, the decorations, the contrast of colors and shapes on each plate, artistic arrangements of outstanding cuisine. Every aspect of a meal was part of a whole, not merely an individual component. It all started in her imagination as one picture, later separated into pieces and recreated amidst participants.

...cinnamon...ginger...slivered almonds...

She could taste each ingredient as she planned its role.

...holly...carnations...baby's breath...eucalyptus...

She could see the colors and textures combining as they came together.

...joy...heartbreak...love...compassion...

She could feel the emotions hovering in the room.

Sometimes she wondered if she thrived on the anticipation of an event as much as the event itself. She loved weaving the empathic aspects of each occasion, the tender piecing together of carefully selected ingredients – culinary, visual, and spatial – into a tapestry of sensations. An apple was not merely an apple. It was fresh air and crisp autumn leaves, a rich sunset, and a child's hand reaching for a cinnamon stick. A ribbon of pasta was wheat in the late afternoon light. It was the tie that bound a family together in joy and grief.

She pulled out a metal container of pastels, dented from years of use. How many shades of red were there in a Christmas memory? How many variations of green in the foliage of faith? Of ivory in a gift's bow? Of blue in the sky of a new year's first day?

A tap on the door brought Mist out of her contemplation. She set her sketching aside and stood, crossed the room and opened the door, surprised to find Betty in the hallway, a worried look on her face.

"The Morrisons are here."

"Now?" Mist's tone was more pensive and curious than it was confused or anxious.

"Yes, now," Betty said. "A day early. Mrs. Morrison apologized profusely. Said she was sure she booked it for tonight."

"She may have," Mist said. "I might have made a mistake when I took her reservation. She only called a few weeks ago. I had just started helping at the hotel."

"No, dear, it wasn't your mistake. She pulled out her confirmation sheet, and it has tomorrow's date. The poor woman feels terrible. Of course, we do have rooms open."

Mist nodded. "Yes, the suite is already set up with fresh linens and towels. I won't have flowers in there until tomorrow. But I can slip some chocolate mints in right now."

"Thank you, Mist. I'll have them fill out the registration card while you do that. Clive is helping bring in their bags right now."

Mist started to close the door as Betty turned away, but stopped as Betty paused.

"We'll need to be very gentle with Mrs. Morrison."

"Of course," Mist said. "I understand she's upset."

"No, not just because of tonight. She's had a very hard year. The whole family has." Betty paused, hearing Clive's voice up front. "Oh, he must have the bags in already."

Mist nodded. "I'll go upstairs to check the suite quickly." She closed the door after Betty left, put away her sketch pad and pastel box, and slipped on a pair of ballet flats. She fastened her hair at the nape of her neck with a seashell clip and left her room, heading to a supply closet in a side hallway.

Betty had always kept individual chocolates on hand for guests. It was a long-standing tradition to place a chocolate on each guest's pillow, a practice Mist continued when she started helping out. But the closet also held other items now, things that she'd collected slowly during the time she'd been at the hotel. Some she'd picked up on supply runs for groceries. Others she'd ordered in, the packages looking no different from incoming art supplies. To anyone else, it might look like an odd assortment of this and that, random items with no connection to the everyday running of the hotel. But to Mist, it was a first aid kit for life.

As Mist pulled chocolate mints from the closet, she could hear Betty reassuring the guests that their early arrival was not a problem – in fact, it was a delightful surprise. Mist smiled as she heard Clive echo Betty's sentiments. They made a good team.

Slipping up a back staircase, Mist entered the Morrisons' accommodations, a suite with two connecting rooms, a king bed in one, a twin in the other. Mist had left the connecting door open when she cleaned the rooms and changed the linens, so that one space flowed freely into the other. Now she made a quick sweep of the suite, turning on miniature Tiffany lamps and placing a chocolate mint on each pillow and a wooden puzzle on the twin bed.

Satisfied the room was ready, she went down the stairs toward the kitchen. She could hear Clive starting up the front steps with the Morrisons' bags.

"Chocolates all set?" Betty was sitting at the kitchen's center table, looking over the registration book and marking the change in arrival date.

"Yes, and I turned lights on for them. Just the small table lamps, so the room wouldn't be dark when they entered."

"You think of everything, my dear."

"If that were true, there would have been flowers in the rooms a day early," Mist laughed.

"Well, I didn't say you were clairvoyant, though at times I've wondered."

Mist smiled, but didn't reply. She'd been told before that she had some type of magic surrounding her. That's what the fortuneteller had said, years ago, when she was barely a teen.

It had been entertaining to others at that particular event, a birthday party for a neighborhood schoolmate. A few people had even grown quiet, nodding in agreement. But she knew it was only a matter of how she perceived the world. Heart wide open. Eyes and ears tuned in.

"Tomorrow morning right after breakfast, I'm picking up the holiday flowers we ordered," Mist said.

"Did someone say 'breakfast?'" As always, Clive managed to materialize at the mention of food.

"Now, Clive, we have extra guests," Betty noted. "You might need to make yourself some toast at that gem gallery of yours. Or, better yet, head on down to Wild Bill's."

Mist almost laughed at the disheartened look on Clive's face, a result of either the anticipated drudgery of dropping bread into a toaster himself or sheer panic at the prospect of breakfast at Wild Bill's.

"Do I have another option?"

"Yes, you do," Mist said. "You can come right over in the morning and have cheddar-herb frittata and fresh banana nut bread. Coffee's ready in the lobby by 6:30, but you know that already, don't you?" She sent Clive a conspiratorial look. It hadn't escaped her attention that the coffee pot was always two inches lower by 6:45, even if no one in the hotel was awake yet. Mist had a back-up coffee pot in the kitchen while she prepared breakfast, so she never touched the one in the lobby.

"Any chance of testing that banana nut bread now?"

"Only if you want raw batter," Mist quipped. "It goes in the oven at 5:45 tomorrow morning."

"I think I can wait."

"I had a feeling you'd say that," Betty laughed.

Mist took the opportunity to excuse herself and retreat to her room. Her sketchpad called. As did the next day.

CHAPTER THREE

The whir of the juicer wasn't enough to drown out the commotion in the lobby. Mist turned off the machine and glanced at the time: *6:45 am*. The loaves of banana nut bread cooled on wire racks, the frittata baked in the oven and, as far as she knew, everyone was still asleep. *Well, obviously not everyone.* She wiped orange pulp off her hands with a kitchen towel and headed for the lobby where she found a young boy sitting in the middle of the floor. His tear-stained cheeks indicated his day was not off to a perfect start. Pieces of the wooden puzzle lay scattered across the lobby floor.

"Hello." A one-word greeting seemed enough, in view of the unknown situation. "I'm Mist," she added.

After a pause, the child looked up and frowned. "So?" He flopped back from a sitting position to lying flat on his back.

Mist smiled, quickly forcing herself to appear serious. After all, it was a serious question he had posed. She sat down on the floor a few feet away and then lay down and stretched out, mimicking his position. Without looking over, she could feel him glance at her curiously.

Fortunately, the frittata had another ten minutes to go, plus she had set the timer. She could afford a few minutes of patience. She closed her eyes and waited. It paid off.

"I'm Robert."

"Hello, Robert." Another minute passed.

"I hate this puzzle. I hate everything."

"Gosh," Mist said. "That must feel awful."

"And everyone."

"Ew, really awful." Another minute passed.

"I'm five years old."

"I'm twenty-eight."

"You're old."

"I suppose so."

A deeper voice cut in. "What do we have here?" Mist looked up to see Clive standing over them both, coffee cup in hand. He wore faded overalls, a flannel shirt and a perplexed look on his face,

"That's Robert."

"That's Mist."

"She's old."

"He hates everything."

"I see," Clive said.

The conversation was short-circuited by a sharp ringing sound from the kitchen. Mist raised herself up to a sitting position and then stood. "Well, Robert, eggs are calling me. It was very nice meeting you." She headed for the kitchen, aware of small footsteps right behind her.

"Eggs don't talk."

Mist turned the timer off and smiled. "You're right, they don't. But they can burn, so stand back." She waited for Robert to move away, then pulled the pans from the oven, setting them on top of the stove.

"Those eggs smell like bananas."

Clive grinned. "I believe the young man has a good nose." He glanced around the kitchen, his eyes landing on the wire racks. "And I'm thinking we'd better investigate his theory, to see if we can find out why."

"In that case, both of you vamoose." Betty shooed them with her hands as she entered the room. "You two can do your investigating in the breakfast room, like everyone else." She paused, taking a closer look at the young boy. "Well, hello, Bobby. My, you've grown."

Robert frowned. "Why do grown-ups always say that?"

Betty looked at Clive, who simply said, "He has some valid points this morning."

"You're lucky," Mist said. "I haven't grown at all." She crossed the kitchen, lifted a loaf of banana nut bread off a wire rack and placed it on a wooden board, carved in the shape of a sleigh.

"No, she hasn't." Betty looked at Mist's slender figure with envy.

Clive laughed, patting his stomach. "Well, I think I have, thanks to Mist. Or no thanks, as the case may be."

"I need a helper," Mist said, facing the group. She cast an innocent look around the kitchen, avoiding eye contact with any one person. "I don't think I can put this on the table in the other room and still finish all my work."

"I'll do it," an eager voice responded. "My kindergarten teacher says I'm a good helper."

"Oh, thank you so much." Mist exhaled a dramatic sigh of relief as she handed the wooden board to Robert. "I guess maybe you don't hate everything if you like being a helper."

"I guess not," Robert said. He shrugged his shoulders. "I only hate some things."

"You had to be there," Clive explained, noticing Betty's confused look.

Mist pulled a large dish of sliced strawberries from the refrigerator, garnishing the edge of the bowl with a sprig of mint. Pouring whipping cream in another bowl, she added a touch of sugar and set about beating it while Betty took the berries to the buffet table, then added a pan of the cheddar-herb frittata. Mist followed a few minutes later, setting the bowl of whipped cream next to the fruit.

Just past 7 a.m., the front door began to open and close as townsfolk sauntered in. Each stopped to drop money into a container near the buffet. Some contributed more, some less. Mist had set a precedent of refusing to price meals. *Leave what your heart tells you*, the sign on the container read. By some mysterious phenomenon, the total always seemed to cover the cost of the food.

Clayton and the fire crew – all two of them – were the first to arrive, as always. Stomping snow off their boots at the door, they hung their jackets in the hall and were hunched over full plates in minutes. Betty made the rounds with coffee, stopping to pour the fresh-brewed roast into pottery mugs of mixed sizes and shapes, made by a local artist who was local only during summer months, when tourists flocked to the small town in search of Old West history and sapphires, a unique feature of the area.

Others arrived, some lingering in conversation, others grabbing something light before heading back out. Maisie stopped in briefly for a glass of orange juice. She waved to Mist and gestured in the direction of her flower shop, quickly exiting with a slice of banana nut bread in her mouth.

"I take it this is the breakfast room now." Sally Morrison stood in the arched doorway from the lobby, husband right behind her. Both surveyed the room, their raised eyebrows and smiles indicating they were impressed.

Betty greeted them, making sure they bypassed the payment container. The room rates covered the morning meal.

"Good morning! Yes, we've made some improvements this year." Betty extended her arm, showing off the room with pride. "Actually, we have a guest chef in residence. That's probably the easiest way to explain our new café. And she paints. You'll see some of her work on the walls."

"And in my gallery," Clive added, beaming a natural salesman's smile. "She's a mighty fine artist. I can barely keep her miniature paintings in stock. Must have sold two dozen of them just this past week. C'mon over after breakfast and take a look around." He indicated two open seats at the table he and Robert shared.

"Bobby, I told you to stay in your room until we all came down together." Sally Morrison looked at her son and frowned.

"My name is Robert." Without looking up, the boy picked up a slice of strawberry from his plate, dipped it in whipped cream, and popped it into his mouth.

"You must be the Morrisons. Would you care for some Java Love?" Mist stood beside the table with a carafe of coffee in one hand. She had approached so quietly that she startled Sally. Mist's unconventional name for coffee undoubtedly threw her, too.

"Don't let her scare you," Clive laughed. "Mist has a way of appearing without warning. Trust me, it's nothing to be afraid of. She just seems to glide when she walks, even with those confounded army boots she wears. Quiet as a church mouse – I think that's the expression."

"Cool," Robert said, looking down and noticing Mist's boots for the first time. "I want some like that."

"You don't need boots, Bobby," his mother said. She nodded to Mist, who filled her coffee mug.

Robert slumped down and kicked the chair legs with his heels.

"Stop that, Bobby," Sally Morrison said, but without much energy. She thanked Mist for the coffee while Robert sat back up.

Clive lifted his coffee mug with a pleading expression. Mist rounded the table and filled mugs for both Clive and Mr. Morrison. "Call me Bob," the father said as Mist greeted him formally.

Mist indicated the buffet table. "Help yourself. I'll be in the kitchen. Just let me know if you need anything."

"You should let me finish up with breakfast," Betty said. "I know you're just itching to get those flowers and start arranging."

Betty was right, of course. Mist had dreamed of flower arranging the night before, hardly able to wait for morning. Although she regularly put petite vases of flowers in guest rooms and a medium-sized display on the registration counter, she had a bigger flower budget than usual for the Christmas holiday, which allowed for more lavish designs.

"If you really don't mind."

"Not at all," Betty said. "Besides, better to get it done before the later check-ins start arriving."

"That's right," Mist said. "Mr. Blanton and Mrs. Winslow."

"Exactly. Now, you run along and take care of whatever you need to get done before tomorrow." Betty said. "I'll finish up here. Then I'll take a stroll down to Marge's place while you work on the flower arrangements."

Mist smiled. Betty's daily stroll to the candy store provided not only a chance to visit with her longtime friend, but also the opportunity to restock caramels, her favorite addiction.

"Thank you so much," Mist said. She was eager to get her hands into decorating. With that in mind, she traded her apron for a ragged sweatshirt with a UC Santa Cruz logo on it, covered that with a pea coat from the local thrift store, and headed out.

CHAPTER FOUR

Maisie's Daisies only opened two days a week during the summer and once a week during the winter, when the shop owner brought fresh flowers down from Helena. This schedule only differed once each year, when Maisie brought an extra batch into town just before Christmas, an ideal setup, as far as Mist was concerned. She'd been able to do light touches several days earlier, but would have fresh flowers and greenery for Christmas Eve and Christmas Day. She'd planned ahead for the floral arrangements, making sure to cover the buffet, the centerpieces on the dining tables, the main lobby and the guest rooms.

"How did you do, Maisie?" Mist entered the small shop with the enthusiasm of a child going toy shopping. "Were you able to get any of the special requests?"

"Most of them, you'll be glad to hear." The petite, plump woman grinned. Her spiked green hair blended in seamlessly with a bucket of ferns and holly right behind her.

Mist looked over the selection, pleased to see large, white spider mums, in addition to branches of eucalyptus, two items she'd been counting on. She set two large bundles of each aside and debated the various red options. Roses were usually too traditional for her taste, but she could use some to add elegance to the buffet. Carnations could serve for volume on the centerpieces, but she combined them with a heavy purchase of red berries, clustered on branches.

"More greenery?" Maisie stood back, as if already knowing what Mist would pick.

"Absolutely," Mist answered. "Just give me a mixture, every type of green you have. Like the floor of a forest after a heavy wind. A mosaic of nature."

"A mosaic of nature." Maisie repeated Mist's words, not to mock, but to contemplate. Mist knew she was used to her unusual orders from other occasions. Like the time just weeks before when she'd asked for a forest fire palate, with the beauty still left in. The Thanksgiving arrangement of burnt orange lilies and dried branches had been exquisite with touches of yellow aster and yarrow.

"Any mistletoe?"

"Sold out, I'm afraid. But maybe you could use something here?" Maisie reached under the counter and pulled out a flat tray, placing it on the counter. Mist's eyes lit up at the sight of tiny pinecones and sticks of cotton, full and fluffy, but still on the branches. The tray also held flat stones, bark, twine and other miscellaneous items.

"These are truly treasures, Maisie. I'll never be able to decide."

"You don't have to," Maisie said. "The tray is for you. I don't sell this type of stuff. I just collected it, thinking – no, make that knowing – that you'd want to do something unusual."

"Unusual is good. It opens up our minds. It's like life, full of unexpected discoveries." Mist rummaged through the tray's contents like another person might explore a jewelry box.

Maisie transferred the rustic treasures into a handled bag, so Mist could easily carry it. "I'll invoice the hotel for the flowers. I've been jotting down the selections as you picked them. Many guests coming this year?"

Mist headed for the exit, her arms filled with a festive display of nature. "Seven hotel guests, but I imagine we'll have a good crowd for dinner."

"Well, I'll be there. And I hope your first Christmas in Timberton will be one of many to come," Maisie said. "You've lifted the town spirits, made people's lives a little better. I suppose that's the reason you're here, if you believe in that kind of thing." She stepped around the counter to hold the shop door open.

"Maisie," Mist said, pausing just a second in the doorway. "That's the reason we're all here."

* * *

When Mist returned, she saw a dark green SUV sitting in front of the hotel. Her first thought, oddly enough, was how well the vehicle's color blended with the foliage in her arms. If not for the chrome and glass, she might even have been able to incorporate it in the holiday décor. The thought made her smile.

"Well, look at all that," Betty remarked as Mist entered the kitchen. "We might not have room for food on the tables once you finishing spreading all that around."

"You'll see," Mist said, setting the flowers and greenery in a bucket, stems down. She moved to the sink, filled a pitcher with water, and poured it into the bucket. "It will all come together – guests, food, decorations, memories and hope."

"That's good to hear," Betty said. "Because this hotel is filling up by the minute. Mr. Blanton arrived while you were out, much earlier than expected."

"His room is ready." Mist pulled a single spider mum from the bucket, contemplating it with fixed concentration.

"I'm sure it is," Betty laughed. "I never worry about the rooms with you here. But I did have him wait in the parlor until you returned, in case you wanted to check the room."

"Just eucalyptus and berries."

"What?"

"The perfect companions to this flower are eucalyptus and berries. Such a wonderful mix of textures, don't you think, Betty?" She pulled a branch of eucalyptus out of the bucket, along with a cluster of berries and held them up together, experimenting with the height of each in relation to each other.

"Well, what do you know? You're absolutely right," Betty said. "I would have just thrown a bunch of those into a vase with red carnations and some fern."

Mist smiled. "That would have been beautiful, too." She set the flower and accompanying branches back into the bucket, washed and dried her hands and headed to the front parlor, where she found the new guest sitting in an armchair, book in hand, just as Betty had described him the night before.

An advantage to her unique way of walking soundlessly, Mist observed him, unnoticed. Seated, it was hard to guess his height, but he appeared tall. Definitely lanky, as evidenced by the angle of one leg dangling over the other. His hair was a medium brown, not short but not long. Only the words in the leather-bound book he held could see his eyes. He held a pencil in one hand, tapping its eraser against his right cheek every few seconds. He wore a pair of brown slacks and a simple, light-green shirt, plain and unremarkable.

"Mr. Blanton?"

The man looked up from the book and paused, not looking around, as if unsure what direction the sound came from. Mist repeated his name a little louder. He turned his head in her direction and smiled. Standing up, he set the book in the chair and crossed the room, extending his hand. She noticed he walked with a slight limp.

"Yes, but please call me Michael."

Now, facing him directly, Mist could see his eyes, yet couldn't pinpoint the color. Was there such a thing as foggy steel green? Not quite brown, not quite green, not quite hazel. Almost grey, but with a touch of...that third chalk stick from the right side of her pastel container.

Mist refocused her attention on greeting the guest, who now looked mystified, as if wondering where she had gone. If only she could explain that she wasn't quite sure herself. There had been many times in the past that she'd wished to do just that, times when a color or texture took her to an alternate consciousness before releasing her from its spell.

"I'm so sorry, I just..."

"They're green-grey, or grey-green, as you wish." He smiled. "Don't worry, they throw everyone off. I don't think there's an actual name for the color, but my mother had the same eyes."

"I see," Mist said, though she didn't see at all. Green-grey or grey-green fell far short as a description. "I believe I would call them patina."

"Patina? Is that even a color?"

"Colors can be many things – light, sound, texture," Mist said, more convinced now that recognition had sunk in. "There's a slight touch of copper in there with the green and grey. Your eyes are patina."

"I'll put that on my driver's license, then, when it comes up for renewal."

"You should," Mist said, pleased to have solved a puzzle. She turned away, retrieving a registration card and pen from the desk, which she handed to the guest. "I believe your room is ready, but I'd like to check it quickly. I'll be right back."

Leaving Mr. Blanton to fill out the hotel card, Mist went to the back hallway closet and perused her options. Flowers would not be ready until mid-afternoon, but she could put out a chocolate mint now. She looked over the shelves of odds and ends and chose a vintage copy of Dylan Thomas's *A Child's Christmas in Wales*. Closing the closet, she made a quick trip up the rear staircase and back. The room was ready.

"Room 14, just up the stairs and to the right. I'll show you the way."

"That's OK. I know where it is."

"Then let us know if you need anything. If I'm not here, Betty will be."

"Thank you. I'm glad to see Betty has help now. She's always worked so hard to run this hotel."

"I only do a few things around the hotel; mostly I run our small café." Mist pointed across the hall. A carved wooden sign with the word "Moonglow Cafe" hung from the arch of the doorway.

"A café here, that's new. Great idea, as a matter of fact. I used to smuggle food in with me, to avoid going to that horrible place down the road."

"Wild Bill's"

"Yes, that's the one!" He shuddered. "Well, whatever you serve here is bound to be great in comparison to those greasy eggs."

"I hope you think so. Perhaps you'll have dinner here tonight and see."

"Are there any other new options in town?"

"Not really."

"Then I'll plan on it."

With that, the guest slung a large duffel bag over his shoulder. Holding onto the banister for support, he headed upstairs, leaving Mist pondering both his limp and the dinner menu.

"Mist, dear?" Betty's voice calling her to the kitchen pulled her mind away from the odd conversation. Had she just completed a check-in with a discussion solely encompassing eye color and greasy eggs?

"Mr. Blanton is getting settled in," Mist said, as she entered the kitchen. "I put him in Room 14, as noted in the registration book." She saw a new bag of caramels on the kitchen's center table and smiled.

"Yes, that's his favorite room," Betty said. "It has a comfortable chair for reading and gets a view of the sunset each evening. He requests the same room each year."

"Where is he from?" It wasn't the eye color that had Mist intrigued, or was it? No, there was something about his overall demeanor. Calm, yet guarded, like a book daring to be opened.

"New Orleans, I believe, though he doesn't have a southern accent," Betty admitted. "His address lists a post office box there."

"We don't always end up where we begin," Mist mused. "There's something familiar about him. Not about him specifically, but the energy around him." She knew Betty wouldn't quite understand this. Even after months of knowing each other, metaphysical philosophy wasn't a subject they discussed. Not that Betty didn't send her questioning looks on occasion. But she was used to that.

"You know best, dear," Betty said.

"I sense a similar energy around the Morrisons. I know you said they've had a tough year."

"Yes," Betty said. "They lost their youngest child last year. I believe it might have even been on today's date. It's the reason they weren't able to be here. They cancelled their reservation at the last minute."

"No wonder there is an aura of sadness around them," Mist said. "We'll have to pull together some holiday joy to help fill the emptiness." Though she had been just a toddler when she lost her parents to a car accident, she'd been eighteen when the grandmother who raised her passed away. She remembered the pain of that loss.

Mist turned to the bucket of flowers and greenery, contemplating the arrangement options silently. The bark-covered containers she'd been constructing over the last few weeks would be just right for each table's centerpiece – not too large to crowd the place settings, they would add a holiday touch to the meal. Her overall vision of the table blended the best of everything the season had to offer. Not the least of which were the guests themselves.

The residents of Timberton were enthralled with her food; she knew that. After all, they hadn't had many options before she arrived. But she also suspected they didn't recognize the true ingredient that made the meals special: the people who sat at the table, who brought their silent dreams and wishes with them. Whether in conversation with each other, or reading a newspaper next to a warm cinnamon roll, those thoughts and feelings were ever present.

"I'll be in the dining room," Mist said.

"You mean the café," Betty laughed. "Don't forget it's your café now, not just another hotel parlor."

"The café belongs to us all," Mist said. "It doesn't belong to me, or to any one person." She smiled, knowing Betty wouldn't disagree with that. Arguing with Mist's view of the world was pointless.

CHAPTER FIVE

Tables cleared, breakfast long over, the café stood before Mist like a blank canvas. Except that it wasn't. She'd rearranged the tables and chairs a week before to match her concept of the holiday meals. Paintings of snow-dusted branches hung on the walls, bringing a touch of the wintery outdoors inside. Garlands of evergreens draped across the upper walls, tiny white lights hidden inside, a secret to be revealed on Christmas Eve.

Mist set to work, weaving tapestries of eucalyptus and pinecones, bursts of floral colors and dry branches, ribbons and bark. As she created, she hummed Christmas melodies she'd known since childhood, the music of memories. Hours flew by. In the end, a magnificent arrangement spanned the center of the buffet, with miniature renditions of the same on each table.

"Mighty fine."

Mist turned to see Clive standing in the doorway, nodding his head with approval. She smiled. It was a far cry from the western art he displayed in his gallery, but he was clearly impressed. That was the thing about holiday decorations. People's hearts could bond over them.

"Good afternoon, Clive. What brings you around today? Wouldn't be a certain lady we both know?" His face reddened like a schoolboy caught kissing a pretty girl under the bleachers.

"You can tease me all you want, young lady," Clive said. "But I'm here to replace a bulb in that entryway chandelier before the cookie exchange this afternoon. I don't want Betty climbing up a ladder. Her hip's been bothering her lately. She won't say so, but I see the way she runs her hand over it when she's been working too much."

"I've seen her do that, too. I'm glad you're here to help her."

"Well, if not me, you'll be climbing those ladders, too. And we don't want that."

"That's sweet of you to worry about me, but I'm strong and don't mind climbing ladders."

Clive laughed. "Oh, I'm not worried about you. I just don't want you falling and breaking an arm. What would we eat? The whole dang town might just starve."

Mist swatted him with a eucalyptus branch and pushed him out of the room. Both laughing, they almost bumped into a woman who stood directly under the chandelier in question. They straightened up quickly, like children just caught misbehaving.

"Welcome to the Timberton Hotel," Mist said, extending her hand. The woman's soft, wrinkled hand slid into her grasp.

Clara Winslow stood no more than five foot two and appeared frail enough that one light gust of wind could blow her clear out of town. Even her winter coat did little to add bulk to her frame. Her left hand held two red mittens, a toast to the season. Snow speckled her dark leather nursing type shoes. It struck Mist as odd the woman wasn't wearing a hat or scarf, as if she didn't care whether the crisp air chilled her face or neck. And then it occurred to Mist: perhaps she *didn't* care. This was the guest who was traveling without her husband for the first time, to spend a holiday at a hotel that had been their favorite for many years. Together, always together.

"Here, let me take your coat," Mist offered. She introduced herself as she helped Mrs. Winslow remove her arms from the wool sleeves. She hung the coat on an antique oak stand in the corner of the front hall. She led her to the desk to fill out a registration card and pick up her room key. As she filled out the required information, the woman glanced around with a mixture of appreciation and sadness.

"I'm happy to be here," Mrs. Winslow said.

"And we're happy to have you here," Mist responded.

"I didn't know if I would be, but I am."

"That's good," Mist said, treading lightly. There was no reason to say anything else. Mrs. Winslow would disclose more if she wanted to.

"This was…oh, never mind. If the room is ready, I'd love to get settled in."

"As a matter of fact, it's ready and waiting for you. Let me show you where it is."

"It's fine, I know where…or, yes, maybe you should show me." The comment didn't take Mist by surprise. Betty's note in the registration book specified not to put Mrs. Winslow in Room 19, the one she and her husband had always shared.

Mist took the key from a cubbyhole on the wall behind the desk and led Mrs. Winslow upstairs. She saw the woman glance toward Room 19 as they turned away from it and headed down a different hallway.

The room Mist had chosen for the widow looked out into a courtyard behind the hotel. Room 16 was light and airy, cheerful even when sunshine had to fight its way through cloud and snow during this winter season. A double bed fit nicely into the space, still allowing room for a sitting area near the window. Mist had switched out the regular bed covering for an Amish quilt with holiday colors. A petite crystal vase held a single white rose and a sprig of holly. Mist had also seen to it that the Tiffany lamp on the bedside table blended with the colors in the quilt.

"My, it's lovely! And that quilt is beautiful. Why, I've never seen anything like it."

"It's a cathedral star pattern, quilted with holiday colors and prints," Mist said.

"It looks like a stained glass window! Everything is perfect, my dear."

"I hope you enjoy the room, Mrs. Winslow. It's filled with sunshine when the weather cooperates. The antique walnut wardrobe is one of my favorite pieces in the hotel."

"Carl would have loved that wardrobe," Clara said. She turned to Mist to explain. "My late husband. I just lost him a few months ago."

"I'm so sorry." Mist's sincerity made Clara smile.

"It's OK, my dear. I almost didn't come to Timberton this year, but I decided I would feel closer to Carl if I came, closer to those wonderful holiday memories." Clara paused, looking around.

"I've left some books on the nightstand for you," Mist said. "If the radiator acts up, just call us right away. It can be temperamental."

"It's perfect. And please call me Clara." She stepped forward unexpectedly and hugged Mist, an impulsive gesture that took them both by surprise. "Thank you."

"You're welcome, Clara. I'll let you settle in. There will be wine, tea and refreshments in the front parlor later this afternoon."

"How wonderful. What time is that?"

"Anytime," Mist whispered. "Betty will tell you five o'clock, but really, it might be anytime." Mist smiled at Clara's quizzical expression as she slipped out into the hall and closed the door.

Mist found Betty and Clive sitting at the center table when she returned to the kitchen. Clive had already finished switching out the light bulb.

"I think everyone's in for the day," Mist said.

"Actually, no, dear," Betty said. "I had calls from both of tomorrow's guests. The weather shows a storm blowing in tomorrow. Ms. Greeley is flying in a day early, to make sure she doesn't get stranded traveling. And Professor Hennessy is driving down from Missoula for the same reason. Seems we'll have a good crowd by tonight."

"Good that they're traveling while it's safe." Mist began recalculating dinner plans in her head. "What time do they expect to arrive?"

"The professor will be here this afternoon. Ms. Greeley won't be in until around dinnertime."

"Two more for dinner will be easy," Mist said. "There's always plenty of food, since I'm never sure how many people will come by. And I do like to have extra for Hollister. On cold nights like this, he usually comes around."

"You take good care of him, Mist."

"We all do," Mist said.

"What's on the menu for tonight?" Clive was always first in line for dinner.

Mist smiled. "We'll just have to see what comes together."

"I smelled bread baking early this morning," Betty said.

"That's always a good sign," Clive said. Mist was certain she heard him smacking his lips as she headed out of the kitchen.

* * *

Marge was the first to arrive for the cookie exchange, bringing a plate of snickerdoodles, which she placed on the buffet. Mist had heard that Marge's cookies were legendary, a town favorite. She eyed them with interest as she set out a pot of freshly brewed coffee. She'd make a point of trying them.

A few minutes later, Maisie arrived, a tub of chocolate chip mint cookies tucked under her arm. She handed Betty the container before taking off her coat, knit cap and thick, emerald green scarf and hanging them on the lobby rack.

"These look decadent, Maisie!" Betty exclaimed. "We'd better watch these carefully. We have a five-year-old chocolate fanatic running around here this year." She added the cookies to the buffet arrangement.

The variety of cookies mounted, one by one, some holiday favorites, others simply beloved family recipes. The owner of the beauty shop brought Melting Moments, a recipe she'd begged a local client for after receiving a batch as a gift one year. Soon after, Millie, the town librarian, showed up with a plate of ginger crackle cookies. She poured a cup of coffee, and joined Betty, who was in conversation with the curator of the local historical society, who had just arrived with a tin of powdered sugar concoctions.

"Cook's Nut Balls, you say?" Betty eyed the tin with delight. "I do believe I'm gaining two or three pounds every time someone walks in."

"That's what the holidays are for, Betty!" Marge laughed.

Three women from the local church choir showed up with almond thumbprint cookies, peanut blossoms, and other decadent treats, each variety looking even more delicious than the one before. Betty, knowing she'd want more than one assorted plate to serve guests for the next few days, contributed four plates herself, just as she'd done previous years. Regulars to the annual cookie exchange knew to expect her usual favorites.

Mist excused herself and left Betty to bask in the glory of this longstanding Timberton custom. Although Betty needed Mist's help running the hotel, she also needed to allow herself to indulge in this tradition without Mist hovering. The cheerful chatter and laughter filling the hotel proved this.

Back in her room, Mist pulled out her sketchpad and thought over the arrangements for Christmas Eve dinner and Christmas Brunch the following day. She never reserved specific seats for meals, but let the diners choose their own tables depending on what felt comfortable. Corner tables, large tables, smaller tables for one or two, and round tables, perfect for group conversation.

Mist felt differently about the upcoming Christmas meals. Although she didn't know the specifics of all the guest's circumstances, she did sense that she might need to offer extra care. Clara Winslow had lost her husband; the Morrison parents had lost a child, Robert a brother. Mist knew that Michael Blanton came to Timberton alone each year, and "alone" was his normal, but something about his limp made her feel this year held a different tone. The visiting professor was away from his family in England. And she knew little about Ellen Greeley, except that there must be a reason behind a trip for two turning into a solo journey. Every guest faced a challenge, even if they didn't realize it.

Picking up a pencil, Mist sketched out place cards for each guest, along with a holiday image for each, something specific she could contribute to the memories of the guests, designs like simple sleds and fir trees, stars and bows, stockings and the outline of a gingerbread man. Christmas memories were special. They became part of their personal life paintings.

Satisfied with her drawings, she set them aside and returned to the kitchen, finding it now empty. Betty had her hands full with the cookie exchange and Clive would be back at his gem gallery, where he spent afternoons working on jewelry designs and hoping customers would come in for last minute gift purchases.

Planning meals for an unknown number of people was a challenge, but Mist always had back-up plans in place. She prepared larger portions than necessary, knowing she could leave leftovers in the spare refrigerator in Room 7. The small room in the back of the hotel remained available for Hollister, just in case he chose the heated space some nights over his colder makeshift home under the railroad trestle. Often enough, the food disappeared and the covers on the twin bed in that room looked adjusted. Mist felt her heart warm each time she saw that the homeless man had accepted the hotel's generosity. The town had come together for the unusual resident, allowing him the choice of comfort, but also the independence he was used to.

Now, Mist pulled the ingredients she needed from the pantry, refrigerator and root storage area. Within an hour, the oven would be filled with culinary magic, with two simmering saucepans above adding fragrant aromas to the mix. Later, she would pass through the café, adjusting tables and setting up the buffet, every detail, aside from the food. Plates, napkins – always cloth, never paper, serving dishes and utensils waited for hungry recipients. Only the food itself would be missing. It would appear at 6 p.m. on the dot, just like it did every night. Almost like magic, the townsfolk often said. Others would call this clockwork.

CHAPTER SIX

Incessant pounding on the front door sent Mist scurrying to the entryway. It was rare that anyone knocked on the door, much less used it for a punching bag. As a hotel, the building was always open to the public. Guests usually walked in on their own, heading for the registration desk. Residents of Timberton considered it a home away from home. They came and went at will, perhaps grabbing a chocolate chip cookie and dropping some change in the collection box.

When Mist opened the door, she found a huffy, red-faced man in his mid-fifties. It was hard to tell whether he was angry or merely cold. Mist's best guess was a little of both. Tips of graying hair peeked out from below a winter hat. He wore wire-rimmed glasses that were steamed up, if not from the weather, then from his indignation. His salt and pepper mustache wiggled as he furrowed his eyebrows and spoke.

"It's cold out here."

"Why, yes it is." A sudden impish urge inside Mist tempted her to remain still, leaving the two statements hovering in the air. Her manners got the upper hand, though. She promptly invited him in.

"I'm Professor Nigel Hennessy. I have a reservation." The man stomped his feet, leaving patches of melting snow on the floor. Mist made a quick mental note to fetch towels as soon as the man filled out his paperwork and headed off to his room. It wouldn't do for the elderly Clara Winslow, or anyone else, for that matter, to slip and fall. Especially not right before holiday festivities.

"Welcome to the Timberton Hotel, Mr. Hennessy," Mist said. "Would you like me to take your coat?"

"*Professor* Hennessy," the man clarified.

Mist repeated the question. "Would you like me to take your coat, Professor Hennessy?"

"No, I would not. I'd like the key to my room. Can't you tell I'm tired and cold?"

Mist was grateful Clive was at the gallery and not in the kitchen, which would have put him within hearing range. Clive was protective of both Betty and Mist. It wouldn't have been beyond him to tell the man he shouldn't have remained outside, pounding on the door, if he didn't want to be cold. Mist smiled to herself. There was a reason Clive wasn't in the hospitality business.

"Let's get you warmed up, then," Mist said, hastening to give him a pen and registration card. "Perhaps I could get you some coffee or tea?"

"Tea, of course," the man huffed. "How you Americans drink that bloody coffee all day is beyond me." He scribbled his information on the card and slapped the pen on the desk, extending his hand for the key. "I'll have the tea in my room."

"Milk or sugar with that?" Mist held the man's room key in one hand, tapping it against her other hand while waiting for an answer.

"Naturally." The professor reached across the counter, snatched the key from Mist's hand, turned and headed upstairs without another word. Mist was amused at his abrupt manner. Though she normally offered to walk guests to their rooms, she hadn't even had the chance to tell him his room number. She stayed behind the desk until the professor came back down the stairs.

"What room does this go to?"

"Room 11, Professor Hennessy, just to the right of the stairs."

"It doesn't say so on the key."

"No, it does not."

"Why?"

"Because if you lose your key and a stranger finds it, that person wouldn't know which room the key belongs to. It's for your safety."

"Well, that's ridiculous. Does that really seem like a good idea to you?"

Mist paused. "I believe I'm the wrong one to ask, Professor. I don't think there should be keys at all, anywhere."

"You're a very strange girl."

"Yes, so I've been told," Mist said, watching the professor go up the stairs.

In the kitchen, Mist opened one of many cabinets she used for special stashes. When it came to beverages, people were particular. This was a matter of habit, personality and preference, all rolled up into one desire for liquid nourishment.

Fifteen minutes later, at precisely 4 p.m., she placed a tray outside Room 11. She tapped on the door and left, quite certain the professor would be pleased with the delivery, though she didn't expect him to say anything. The spread of PG Tips tea, with teacup, saucer, milk, sugar and teapot of boiling water was sure to delight the persnickety Brit. If not, the accompanying tin of McVitie's digestives and plate of cucumber finger sandwiches would.

Betty was seated at the kitchen's center table when Mist returned downstairs, an empty plastic wrapper in front of her.

"Caramel?" Betty offered.

"No thanks," Mist said. "I just had an unexpected cucumber sandwich."

"An unusual afternoon snack," Betty mused. "I'll stick with my caramels. What brought on the cucumber?"

Mist smiled. "Our English professor. He arrived in need of a little defrosting."

"Oh, dear."

"He'll be fine," Mist laughed. "I think the holidays must be hard for him because he's here alone, away from home. We'll make him feel comfortable."

"You're a miracle worker, you know that, Mist?" Betty unwrapped another caramel and popped it in her mouth, then stood, throwing away both wrappers.

"I appreciate the kind words, Betty, but we can't work miracles in other people. They have to work them within themselves. All we can do is be supportive. If Professor Hennessy defrosts, it will be his choice, not because I brought him a tray of tea, biscuits and finger sandwiches."

"You gave him biscuits, too?"

Again, Mist smiled. "Well, I didn't say we couldn't help push the miracles along."

"Did someone say frosting?"

Both women turned to see Robert standing in the doorway, eyebrows raised. He clutched the wooden puzzle in his hand and surveyed the kitchen, presumably on the lookout for cupcakes.

"Hi, Robert," Mist said. "Sorry, no frosting here. But we'll have cookies after dinner."

"I wanted something now."

"How about some cucumber?" Betty teased. When Robert rolled his eyes and left, both Mist and Betty laughed.

Betty retired to her room for her afternoon ritual rest, which was designed more to let Mist have full reign over the kitchen as she finished dinner preparations than it was to rescue Betty's feet. Although Mist didn't want people to feel unwelcome when she was working, she relished the solitude of the last hour before dinner when she could put all of her energy into cooking.

At 6 p.m. sharp, Mist set a large pan of lasagna on the buffet, next to a mixed green salad and side dishes of zucchini-tomato casserole and garlic-sautéed French green beans. Loaves of sourdough bread baked that morning filled a basket at the end of the buffet.

The usual local suspects filed through within the first fifteen minutes, as was their pattern. Clayton and his crew were in and out the door first. Clive also finished the meal quickly, but lingered to visit with Betty and to help with dishes, something he never heard the end of from the other guys around town.

Bob Morrison came down for dinner with Robert, choosing a table close to the buffet. Mist poured water with lemon into a glass for each, then moved to fill a third at an empty place just beside them.

"Thank you, but that one's not necessary," Bob said, holding up his hand to stop Mist. "My wife isn't feeling well. She won't be joining us tonight."

"She never does stuff with us anymore," Robert said. He grabbed his silverware off the table and sent it clattering to the floor. It landed beside Mist's foot. She picked it up quickly to avoid a potential standoff between father and son over who should pick it up. Other diners were already starting to notice.

"Thank you," Bob said to Mist before turning to Robert. "You need to behave. And it's not true that your mother never does things with us. She's here on this trip."

"She didn't even want to come here! I heard her crying and yelling before we left home!"

Bob gave Mist an apologetic, discouraged look.

"Robert," Mist said, moving a little closer to the boy. "We all get mad and cry and yell sometimes. I know I do."

"You do?" Robert raised one eyebrow, an unexpected, inquisitive gesture that made Mist fight to stay serious. To top it off, she found herself at a loss to provide an example. It had seemed like the right thing to say, yet her response to anger was usually to close her eyes, take deep breaths, and imagine a flock of birds, each representing a frustration, flying off until they disappeared over the horizon.

"You remember how mad you were at the wooden puzzle yesterday?" Mist watched Robert contemplate the question and then nod his head. "Are you still mad at the puzzle?"

Robert shook his head from side to side. "No. It's a cool puzzle."

"You see? I think you'll find your mom is happy to be here with you and your dad. Maybe today she just needs to rest."

"Maybe," Robert said, his focus already moving from the discussion to the lasagna. Calmer, he accepted new silverware from Mist and started in, eating a hefty serving of lasagna and the minimum amount of veggies required to earn his father's permission for a warm brownie afterwards.

There was no sign of the professor all evening, but Clara Winslow and Michael Blanton entered the café at the same time and chose to eat together. Though Mist couldn't hear their conversation, it looked amiable and polite from the door of the kitchen – not overly animated, yet not uncomfortable. At one point, Clara reached across the table and touched Michael's hand. He had brought a book with him, which he'd set aside and later took into the front parlor, along with a cup of coffee.

Over the last few dishes, Clive looked out the window above the kitchen sink and turned to Mist and Betty, who now sat at the kitchen table. Mist was wrapping up leftovers to take to the refrigerator in Room 7 and Betty was working her way through a second brownie.

"I don't like the looks of it out there," he said. "The wind has picked up, and we're starting to get some flurries. Don't you have another guest due tonight?"

Betty nodded, concerned. "One more, the woman from Arizona. What time is it?"

"Half past seven," Mist said.

"She should have been here by now." Betty pushed the brownie away, worried. "In fact, she should have been here a good hour ago. She was going to come in by bus. That bus usually comes through town around 6:30."

Clive put down the kitchen towel after drying the last dish. "I'm going over to Pop's Parlor to ask the bartender if the bus came in. He always gets a few customers when it arrives. He'll know." Grabbing his jacket, hat and gloves, he took off.

"I hope she didn't get caught in the weather," Betty said. "The whole reason she was coming in a day early was to avoid that."

"Maybe she only made it part way, missed a connection or something and will be here tomorrow morning."

"I'd rather see her make it tonight," Betty said. "The weather is just going to get worse."

Mist reassured Betty. "Don't worry. She'll be here tonight." She hoped she was right.

CHAPTER SEVEN

Michael Blanton sat in the armchair next to the fireplace, a copy of Charles Dickens' *A Tale of Two Cities* in his lap, unopened. His head rested on the back cushion of the well-padded chair, his eyelids closed, not a glimpse of patina visible. His breathing was soft, but not silent. For the first time, Mist saw traces of worry in the creased lines of his forehead.

She moved to the front curtains, looking out at the street. Still no sign of Clive or the late arrival. The flurries began to change into a light snow shower, and Mist grew worried.

What she felt wasn't just concern that the last guest was safely on her way; it was like a heavy fog, like something almost tangible that she couldn't quite identify. It filled the hotel, subduing the cheer of the holiday decorations, dimming their brightness. Each guest had brought along a type of sadness, some clear, others unknown. And the combination of it all weighed heavily in the air. Mist could feel it in Clara Winslow's soft handshake, could sense it in the professor's unease. She could read it on Michael Blanton's forehead and hear it in Robert's angry young voice.

At least all this emotion had pooled together under the roof of the hotel, where the burdened guests might find relief in companionship and might even give hope to each other.

Mist turned away from the window at the sound of a dull thud. Michael Blanton had shifted in his sleep, sending Charles Dickens to the floor. Fortunately, a thick rug broke the fall, causing harm to neither one city nor the other, and leaving the reader in slumber. Mist crossed the room, picked up the book, and was setting it on a side table when a voice posed a question.

"It's the way it is, don't you think?"

Michael Blanton's eyes met Mist's, then glanced at the book, then looked up again. Not for the first time, Mist could see something in the tones of grey, green and copper that moved her in an undefined way. She knew what the guest meant.

"The best of times, the worst of times," she said.

"Exactly." Michael rested his head against the chair's back cushion and closed his eyes again.

"They do go together, it seems," Mist said, knowing he wasn't asleep.

"I wonder why that is."

"Because it's life, Mr. Blanton," Mist said. "Life is a mix of situations and emotions."

"You must call me Michael, I insist." A pause. "And I don't believe I know your name at all."

"It's Mist."

The eyes opened again, taking in Mist's face in a pensive manner. "Just Mist? Like fog?"

"I hope not."

"Then like mistletoe, I imagine." A faint smile crossed the guest's face.

"I suppose so," Mist said. "At least at this time of year."

"Come to think of it, I haven't seen any mistletoe among all these beautiful decorations."

"Our flower shop sold out, unfortunately," Mist said. "I'm hoping she'll get more in tomorrow, but I doubt it. They'll close early, since it's Christmas Eve. And they'll be closed Christmas Day, of course."

"This is your first Christmas here," Michael pointed out. "It's a beautiful place to spend the holidays. I come here every year, and it feels like home."

"I imagine it does," Mist replied. "Especially since you've made Timberton your seasonal destination for so long. This clearly is your Christmas home. And where is home the rest of the year?"

"New Orleans," Michael said. "Though I've moved around a lot this year."

Mist didn't press the issue, remembering the post office box Betty had said he used for his registration card.

Clive interrupted the conversation as he hustled through the front door, his hat and shoulders covered with snow.

"Tell Betty the bartender said the bus wasn't coming in tonight. Some kind of mechanical problem. He called the depot and they said some passengers rented cars to get wherever they were headed."

"So you think Ms. Greeley is on her way here by car?" Betty had stepped out of the kitchen at the sound of Clive's voice.

"That's my guess," Clive said. "And the streets are getting bad. I'm going to head up the road and see if I can find her. If she has any kind of car problems, she'll be in trouble."

"And there's no cell access on a long stretch of that highway," Betty said.

"Don't you worry now, Betty," Clive said. "It's a straight shot from town. Pretty hard to get lost. I'm just worried about the weather, plus the fact it's so isolated."

"You be careful, you understand?" Most of Betty's words fell against the inside of a closed front door. Clive had hurried off after his last statement.

"He'll be fine, Betty." Mist's voice was strong and calm. "Clive's old truck is sturdy and dependable. And he knows that road inside out." She turned her attention back to Michael, who'd been listening to the discussion.

"A guest?"

Mist nodded. "Yes, the last guest of the evening. She should have been here already. She was booked for tomorrow, but was trying to get in a day early, to avoid the storm."

"Well, I hope she makes it," Michael said. "This hotel is the perfect place to hide out during a storm. Being here almost makes it seem like there's no storm at all."

"There are often storms inside, as well as outside," Mist said.

Michael's expression didn't change at Mist's declaration. Instead, he agreed. "Yes, you're right."

Robert appeared in the doorway, followed by Clara Winslow, who was dressed in a pale yellow house gown with matching slippers. Robert held a deck of cards. For years,

Betty had made a practice of keeping a deck of cards in each room.

"Over here," Robert said, pointing at a square table in the corner.

Clara followed, smiling at Mist and apologizing for her casual dress. "I was just about to go to sleep when this young man knocked on my door and invited me to play a game of...I believe he called it 'Stupid Fish.'" She winked, which struck Mist as incredibly cute coming from an elderly woman.

"Are any of the fish smart, Robert?" Mist asked.

"Maybe," Robert said, climbing into the chair knees first, an awkward technique typical for his age. Clara slid delicately into the opposite chair, readying herself for the game.

"Tea for anyone? I was about to boil some water. There's decaf coffee on the buffet, if anyone cares for some."

"And cookies!" Robert added. Mist noticed a smidgen of chocolate just to the side of the boy's mouth.

"Yes, you're right, Robert," Mist said. "Do you know how many different kinds?"

"Lots and lots," Robert said.

Michael stood up. "Well, in that case, I think I need to go investigate." He headed for the buffet table.

When Mist turned, she was surprised to see Professor Hennessy standing at the bottom of the stairs holding the tray Mist had left at his door earlier. The tray was empty even of the English biscuit tin. This is exactly what she'd intended, that he keep the tin in his room.

"Professor Hennessy," Mist said. "I'm about to boil some water for tea. Would you like some?"

The man nodded, far calmer than earlier. "That would be brilliant."

Mist headed to the kitchen, to find Betty already putting the water on the stove.

"I overheard you talking about tea. Thought I'd get a head start on it."

"Thanks," Mist said, "I'm going to reheat what's left over from dinner, too. Ms. Greeley is bound to arrive hungry."

"I don't think Professor Hennessy or Sally Morrison came down to dinner, either," Betty added.

Mist smiled. "I think the professor will eat something now."

Ten minutes later, tea and coffee graced the buffet area in the café, an assortment of dishes from dinner nearby. Before long, the professor had served himself a plate of food. At Mist's suggestion, Robert took a plate up to his mother's room. He returned quickly, not about to pass up the chance for a second meal. Clara sat at the table with both of them; Robert had grabbed her hand and dragged her into the café at the announcement of more food. She sipped a cup of tea, making one additional trip to the buffet and back for sugar, which she promptly handed to the professor.

Now it was just a matter of waiting for Clive to return with the last guest.

CHAPTER EIGHT

An hour passed before Clive returned. He appeared tired, but still proud to escort an exhausted looking woman inside. Everyone waiting in the parlor began to applaud the surprised guest as if she were a celebrity. Clive promptly helped remove her coat, then took off his own, hanging them both on the lobby coat rack.

Ms. Greeley was of medium height and weight, with a chin-length mop of brown curls and not a speck of makeup. She wore lightweight tan slacks and a pair of boots not quite fit for snow. A chunky necklace of turquoise beads flopped over the neckline of a black sweater.

"Thank heavens you made it here, dear," Betty said, rushing out from the kitchen. "This is no night to be stuck anywhere."

"I'm glad to be here," the guest said, looking visibly relieved. "I tried to call, but there was no cell service."

"Blowout," Clive explained. "About twenty miles north of here."

"Were you able to change the tire? Oh, my!" The thought of Clive having to work out in such weather hit Betty.

"No, there was no point," Clive said. "The blowout sent Ms. Greeley's car into a ditch. She's lucky it didn't roll. The rental company is sending a tow truck to pick it up."

"Oh, my!" Betty repeated. "Should we try to get Doc over here?"

"No, there's no need," Ms. Greeley said. "I'm not hurt. Just a bit shaken up. I'm not used to traveling alone; in fact, I'm used to someone else doing the driving."

"You were lucky," Clive said. "A blowout is dangerous in any weather. But out here, on a night like this…well, I'm just glad I found you. I knew when that bus didn't come in that something was wrong."

"There were only a handful of us who'd planned to take it. A few stayed in town and others rented cars, anxious to get where they were going. I just wanted to be done traveling."

"We're glad you made it, Ms. Greeley," Mist said. "Why don't you have a seat in the café? Have some hot coffee or tea while I get your registration card from the desk. Help yourself to some food, too, if you haven't eaten."

"It's Ellen, please, and I haven't had a bite to eat since this morning. I'll take you up on that offer right now."

Mist grabbed the card from the front desk while Ellen Greeley headed into the café, filled a plate from the buffet and took a seat. Mist set the card beside the guest, with a pen. "Please take your time. Food is more important than paperwork."

Ellen nodded, a forkful of salad halfway to her mouth. "This salad is exceptional. What is in it, besides pears, which I can taste right away? Oh, and walnuts."

"Not much more," Mist said. "Just an assortment of greens, including arugula, and some sliced beets. The dressing is a white balsamic vinaigrette, a recipe from a restaurant where I worked when I lived in Santa Cruz."

"Well, it's delicious. Not quite like any dressing I've ever tasted."

"It's the thyme," Mist offered.

"What time?"

"No," Mist smiled. "Not time, but thyme, the spice. Just a touch of it makes a big difference."

"Is this a secret recipe?"

"There are no secrets in my kitchen," Mist said. "I believe in sharing food, including recipes, so everyone can enjoy it. What good would it do to keep someone from recreating those same tastes in the future?" She smiled. "I'll let you enjoy your meal. I'll be in the other room when you're ready for your room key." Leaving Ms. Greeley to her food, Mist returned to the kitchen, where Betty and Clive were deep in discussion.

"She could have been killed," Clive said, shaking his head. "When I saw that car in the ditch, I was terrified. It must have been at a forty-five degree angle."

"It's amazing she wasn't hurt," Betty said. "I bet she'll be plenty bruised tomorrow."

"I think you're right," Mist said. "I'll move her to Room 23. She was penciled in for 14, but 23 has that claw foot tub. She'll be able to soak. It'll help her muscles and calm her nerves. I'm sure she's still rattled from the blowout."

Mist stopped by the hallway closet and then slipped up the back staircase, placing a basket of bath oils and fresh lavender next to the tub in Room 23. She fluffed the pillows and added extras, in case Ms. Greeley felt a need to prop up her feet. Moving a vase of holly and white mums from Room 14 to 23, she retraced her steps, arriving in the front hall just as Ellen Greeley placed her registration card on the counter.

"Don't let me leave here without that dressing recipe."

"I won't," Mist promised. "You're here three nights now, right?" Mist looked over the guest book.

"Yes, thank you for letting me add tonight to my stay," Ellen said.

"I'm glad we did," Mist replied. "This storm is pretty fierce now that it's here. Let me show you to your room." She handed a key to Ellen and led her up the stairs. By the time she had the guest situated and had returned downstairs, she felt her own fatigue setting in. She poked her head in the kitchen and told Betty and Clive she was going to bed. The next two days would be busy. Tonight she would rest.

* * *

Mist rolled over onto her side, the cool cotton of her pillow soothing her skin. Half awake, half asleep, she thought at first she heard the soft cooing of doves outside, mixing with the wind. Rising and looking out her window, though, she saw nothing but snow tumbling down, silent. Yet the sound continued from somewhere inside the hotel. She wrapped a tattered silk kimono around her, a favorite she'd received long ago from an exchange student at the university. Barefoot, she slipped out of her room and followed the sound. As she got closer, she could hear tearful, whispered words.

"I wish you were here, Carl. All those years we spent together, we never went anywhere without each other. It's odd, I feel guilty being here without you, yet I couldn't bear the thought of sitting at home. This was always our holiday treat."

Mist stayed back; she didn't need to enter the front parlor to know Clara Winslow was sitting in front of the tree. The lights of the hotel Christmas tree were left on at night, in case guests wandered downstairs for a cookie, or sought quiet time in front of the sparkling lights and old-fashioned ornaments.

After a few muffled sniffles, Clara continued. "Bob and Sally are back this year, without Joshua. You remember they lost him last year. They're changed, hardly the same family. Little Robert has grown, but is angry. Sally barely comes out of her room. And Michael is here, but...oh, Carl, he's had such a tough year. There are new guests, too, people we never met, but they must have stories, too. I wish...well, I just wish, that's all."

Mist tiptoed back to her room, already feeling uneasy that she'd heard as much as she had. Her first instinct had been to approach Clara to comfort her. But it was evident that the private conversation the widow was having would be a greater comfort. She also knew that sometimes, alone in the middle of the night, came the greatest clarity.

The storm had become more intense. Looking outside her room's window, she saw the wind blow snowflakes sideways, weighing branches down unevenly and building drifts against the outer walls of the building. It was good that Ellen Greeley had arrived a day early, good that everyone now rested safely in the hotel.

With Christmas Eve's dawn only a few hours away, Mist lit the kerosene lantern and sat in front of her easel. Using a clamp system that Clive had designed for her miniature paintings, she placed a tiny, framed canvas inside, securing it. Arranging her brushes and varied supplies beside her, she began to paint.

CHAPTER NINE

Mist's painting had eased her into the day, so she was awake early and had plenty of time to put out breakfast before the guests began to come downstairs. She'd done much of the food prep during the previous few days. Now, she only needed to piece everything together – that, and accept help. She'd been delighted when Clive offered to flip pancakes on the griddle. She prepared the batter – a combination of gingerbread, pecans and currants – and he did the labor. Betty took each platter into the café as he stacked it full of the light, fluffy cakes.

Aside from the hot pancakes, the breakfast buffet for the morning of Christmas Eve was simple. A mixture of raspberries, blueberries and strawberries filled one tray, and a chafing dish held scrambled eggs with fresh herbs. The usual assortment of juices, coffee and tea completed the selection. It was enough to start the day and to hold everyone over until the evening meal. No lunch would be served, so hotel staff encouraged guests and townsfolk to eat heartily and to take a muffin or two on their way out. After breakfast, Mist would close the doors to the cafe to decorate and arrange everything for the more extravagant evening meal.

"Here, Mom, sit here! We're having pancakes!" Mist peeked out from the kitchen at the sound of Robert's voice. She was delighted to see his mother joining the family for breakfast. Clara and Ellen Greeley also sat at the Morrison's table.

Professor Hennessy fixed a plate and took it to his room. Mist followed with a tray of tea, leaving it outside his door and tapping lightly before walking away. She made sure to use the same cup and saucer that had soothed him the day before.

Michael Blanton also filled a plate and chose to eat in the front parlor in what was clearly his favorite chair. The Dylan Thomas book that Mist had left in his room replaced his Dickens book from the night before.

Mist cleared the buffet after the breakfast crowd dwindled away. Betty and Clive insisted on doing the dishes, pushing Mist out of the kitchen for a short break before she had to start cooking and decorating. Resigned to being banned from work temporarily, she found herself in the doorway to the front parlor, taking in the scene.

The hotel's Christmas tree sat in front of a large window that faced the street where both guests inside and people passing by outside could enjoy the seasonal cheer of the evergreen. She'd always marveled at what people thought made Christmas trees beautiful, whether the trees were formal with simple colored glass balls or overwhelmed with clumps of tinsel and heavy ornaments that pulled branches toward the floor.

In contrast, as far as Mist was concerned, the Timberton Hotel's tree was perfect. The white lights sparkled just enough to create an air of fantasy, as if the tree itself might work holiday miracles, each tiny light a spark of imagination. Old-fashioned ornaments ranged from wooden toy carvings to crystal angels to handmade creations by the town's schoolchildren, many made at a holiday art workshop that Mist had held earlier in the month. A few were heirlooms going back to Betty's childhood. And Clive had designed a small silver tree that dangled from a higher branch, topped with one of the area's well-known Yogo sapphires. Clive had slipped it on the tree one evening when Betty was out of the room, and she hadn't yet noticed it.

Outside, snow outlined the windowpanes, creating a perfect backdrop for the tree. That evening, Mist would set out bowls of popcorn and fresh cranberries on a nearby table for those who chose to sit around the fireplace and string garlands.

Below the lowest branches, a handmade tree skirt circled the floor, sewn from velvet remnants Mist had found at the thrift store. Wrapped packages in festive holiday colors covered the varied shades of green fabric.

"It's a beautiful tree."

Mist stepped all the way into the room to join Michael, who still sat in that favorite chair.

"Thank you," Mist said. "It's a reflection of the town. Everyone chipped in somehow, whether they provided an ornament or were just present while we decorated."

"You have a wonderful community here."

"We really do," Mist agreed. She wandered across the room toward Michael. "Do you need anything? A refill of Java Love? I'm planning to fix some hot cider for later, but I could do that for you now."

He shook his head. "I'm fine, thank you. There's nothing more relaxing than sitting in a comfortable chair, with a good book. Don't you agree?"

"Absolutely," Mist said, without hesitation. "Though I would have to add painting up there, too. When I paint, the world disappears; it's as if I've stepped into the painting itself. It's almost like magic."

Michael laughed. "Well, now that's something we certainly don't have in common. I tried to paint when I was young, and it was nothing less than a disaster. I remember wanting desperately to paint a rocking horse with a red scarf around its neck. Yet, by the time I added what I thought was a tail, a mane and runners, it looked just like an octopus with ketchup on its head."

Mist tried to hold back her grin but couldn't. This made Michael laugh harder, starting a chain reaction that soon had Mist uncharacteristically bent over with laughter. She sat down in a chair across from him and fanned her face with one hand. Silver bracelets around her wrist chimed. "It sounds like you should stick to reading."

"Yes, I believe you're right," he said. Mist noted that the snow-filled light from the front window accentuated the coppery coloring in his eyes. For a split second, something unspoken passed between them.

"What a delightful tree!" The sudden declaration came from Clara Winslow, who came through the front door, several small bags clasped in her hands. Mist recognized the bags' logos as being from the candy store. "I was admiring it from the front walkway."

"Thank you," Mist said. "We were just saying the exact same thing." She stood up. "Please sit." When Clara started to refuse, Mist made it clear she needed to get moving, anyway. "Unless you all want frozen dinners tonight, you'll need to entertain yourselves for the rest of the day. I'll be putting out hot mulled cider later this afternoon on the registration counter in the lobby."

"That sounds lovely, dear," Clara said, removing her coat and accepting the chair across from Michael. "I'm looking forward to it."

"Save some room for appetizers, too." Mist glanced at Clara's bags and smiled. "I'm making baked Brie puffs."

"Don't worry," Clara laughed. "These are for the trip home. I can't resist that peppermint bark Marge sells at Christmas. I always have to stock up. The Morrisons and Ms. Greeley are down there, too. I imagine all your guests will be heading out with Timberton treats."

"Not me," Robert shouted. He had run through the front door in time to hear Clara's last statement. He zoomed across the front hallway and started up the stairs. "I'm eating all mine."

"One's enough for now," Sally said. "Let's save some for later. Let me have the rest."

"Not fair," Robert said. He came back downstairs and handed the bag of candy to his mother, bumping into Michael's outstretched leg in the process. Michael groaned, causing Clara to throw a worried look in his direction. Sitting down in front of the tree, Robert stuffed a single piece of candy in his mouth before picking up presents to shake, one by one.

"Are you OK?" Clara said.

"Yes, Clara, don't worry," Michael said. "Like I told you, they think they got it all." He turned to see Mist watching the exchange. "I had a tumor removed recently. It's just a little sore still. Nothing to worry about."

Mist nodded and didn't press for more information. Instead, she checked the clock and retired to her room, leaving the guests to enjoy visiting with each other. She had a good hour left before she needed to start preparing dinner, just enough time to add final touches to her artwork from the early morning hours.

CHAPTER TEN

Mist looked over her palette, surveying the various shades. Bright red, forest green and sienna brown waited to join the artistic chorus of her efforts. Cornflower blue and a sweet, soft ivory also stood in line, ready to contribute. The paint gave little of itself, yet the colors offered much. Art was just that way, Mist reminded herself. A little could go a long way.

These tiny squares of stretched canvas, no more than four inches square, would become part of each person's journal, part of an emotional cloth. After two hours, with short pauses to get things going in the kitchen, she sat back, satisfied with the results of her work.

Mist turned her full attention to the day's main task, feeding a crowd of people. She'd set the place cards on one large table to make sure hotel guests could sit together. For the townsfolk, she'd stuck to open seating so they could come and go at different times. This way the tables would turn over, allowing plenty of seating for the anticipated record crowd.

Mist tended to prefer lighter foods such as vegetables, fruits and whole grains, though now and then Betty tried to fatten up her waif-like figure with heavier foods. But Mist cooked to please her guests, and for this festive occasion, she'd planned a menu to satisfy every possible palate. And variety! Guests would be able to skip half the offerings and still waddle out stuffed at the end of the night.

She peeked in the oven. The brown sugar glazed ham baked side by side on the top rack with a standing rib roast, the latter draped in rosemary, garlic, and thyme. On the lower rack, she would place a pan of roasted root vegetables. The timing would be tricky, even with the second oven Clive had installed when they first opened the café. Although she preferred to serve straight from stove to table, feeding a large crowd required compromise, so she'd prepared a few dishes in advance to reheat at the last minute.

"How can I help?" Betty sat at the center kitchen table. Foil-covered pans and napkin-lined empty baskets filled most of the surface. Mist had two special breads planned for the evening meal: roasted garlic sourdough and kalamata olive bread with oregano, both freshly baked that morning.

"I think it's under control," Mist said. "How about just relaxing and keeping me company? Tell me what the guests have been up to. What have I missed while I've been hiding out in the kitchen?"

Betty beckoned Mist toward the kitchen window. "Well, you're missing something now, that's for sure. Come look."

Mist joined Betty at the window just in time to see Robert land a solid snowball hit on Clive's back. Clive tried to retaliate, but missed – probably on purpose.

"Robert looks delighted to have one-upped Clive." Betty grinned.

"Naturally," Mist said. "Clive is a clever man."

"Looks like the professor and Clara bundled up and took a walk together. I bet they're headed down to the candy store."

"Maybe in search of more peppermint bark," Mist said. "Speaking of sweets, do we need to put more glazed cinnamon walnuts out? That bowl keeps emptying quickly."

"No, I refilled it earlier and moved it just high enough to be out of Robert's reach." Betty laughed. "Seems this batch is lasting longer than the last one."

"I'm not surprised," Mist said. "I'm glad the storm let up enough for the guests to spend some time outside."

"The snow's still coming down, but not as heavy as earlier and the wind's not too bad. I especially think it's good for Robert to get out, even for just a bit. Michael is reading in the front parlor and Sally and Bob Morrison are playing cards at the game table." Betty peeked inside one of the foil trays and then covered it back up.

"Beets, carrots, rutabagas, parsnips, radishes and fingerling potatoes." Mist answered Betty's question before she asked. "With a little balsamic vinegar, basil and olive oil."

"And this tray?"

"Brussel sprouts with cranberries, pumpkin seeds and Romano cheese."

"And this one?"

"Wild rice with mushrooms and almonds."

"You're not going to let anyone go hungry, are you? This is one spoiled town," Betty said, shaking her head. "And my regular hotel guests have no idea what a treat they're in for."

"Oh, there is something you can do, after all," Mist said. "I have cucumbers in the crisper that you could cut, if you'd like. Everything else is ready to mix into a tossed salad except that."

"How about dessert?" Clive said. Mist and Betty turned to see him standing in the kitchen doorway, Robert beside him.

"Yeah, what about dessert?" Robert echoed.

"We'll have a special holiday dessert," Mist said, thinking of the Yule Log she'd prepared ahead of time.

"Cake?" Robert's eyes scanned the kitchen, looking for any sign of sweets.

"You're very close," Mist said. "We're having a *Bûche de Noël.*"

"A bush?" Robert exclaimed, clearly disgusted. "We're having a bush for dessert?"

Mist smiled. "No, not a bush. A *bûche*. It's a type of cake that looks like a log. It's a traditional Christmas dessert, especially in France."

"Sounds weird." Robert crossed his arms and frowned.

"Sometimes unfamiliar food does sound weird before you try it," Mist said. "But that's how you discover new things to like."

"Or maybe not like," Robert countered.

"That's always possible. But if you don't try anything new, you'll miss finding some of life's good surprises."

"Well, you can count me in," Clive said, rubbing his hands together. "Any kind of cake is just fine with me, no matter what you call it."

"Fine with me, too." Robert looked up at Clive.

"I take it you're talking about those lumpy things you've got over at my place, in the fridge," Clive said. "I was starting to think someone had chopped down a tree and stored the branches. I was about to toss them in the gallery's wood stove and start a fire until I realized they were covered in chocolate."

"I could eat a whole tree if it's chocolate." Robert's eyes brightened.

"Then you'll like this one," Mist said.

"Yay, a chocolate tree!" Robert took off, running through the hotel.

"Speaking of fires, Clive, how would you like to get one going in the front parlor?" Betty voiced her suggestion with a sweet "honey do" tone. "Be sure to put the grate in front of it. And give Robert a talk about fire safety."

"Excellent idea," Mist said. "That will give the fire a good start before dinner guests arrive. But please don't use the *Bûche de Noël.* There's plenty of firewood on the porch."

"As you wish." Clive grinned and left the room.

"He's a keeper, Betty." Mist said. "I'm glad you two finally figured out you were meant for each other."

Betty laughed. "That makes two of us. I guess sometimes it takes people a few years to figure out their feelings. With us, it just took a few more."

"About four decades, would you say?"

"That's about right," Betty said. "I guess we wasted a lot of years."

Mist shook her head. "I don't see it that way. Your experiences during those years made you who you are. This is simply the right time for you to be together."

"I wish I could see the world through your eyes," Betty sighed. "Everything makes sense to you. It all seems so clear. At least it's clear when you explain it."

"I just see what my senses perceive," Mist said. "And I feel what my heart tells me. It's a matter of listening deep inside myself while watching outside. When you put listening and watching together, it becomes clear."

Betty shook her head, but smiled. "If you say so." She gathered up a pile of cut cucumbers and placed them in a bowl. "Ready to mix."

Mist turned her head toward the kitchen door at the sound of a knock.

"You ladies are working so hard, maybe you should assign a task to me." Michael leaned in the doorframe favoring his healing leg.

"You're a guest, Michael," Betty said. "You know by now I won't let guests do any work."

"I thought you had a task," Mist said.

"Oh, and what exactly would that be?"

"To sit by the fireplace and read." Mist turned her head away, unsuccessfully trying to hide a smile.

"I hardly consider that a task," Michael laughed. "I meant something to help out."

"You don't think that's helping out?" Mist took a challenging stance, one hand hip-level on her forest green batik skirt, the other holding a wooden spoon. "Seeing you in the room, relaxing by the fireplace, tells other guests to do the same. You're inviting them to enter and relax."

"I never thought of it that way," Michael admitted. "I finished Dylan Thomas. Short piece, as I imagine you already know."

"There's a copy of *The Great Gatsby* on the bookshelf to the right of the fireplace." Mist waved the spoon toward the front room.

Michael folded his arms, getting comfortable. "I've read it."

"How about *The Sun Also Rises?*"

"Read it."

"*Brave New World?*"

"Read it."

"*The Call of the Wild?*"

"Read it."

"*A Day in the Life of Flanagan McBean?*"

Michael paused briefly. "Read it."

Mist laughed. "No you haven't. There is no such book."

Michael grinned and backed out of the kitchen. Mist tried to ignore a comical look on Betty's face.

"I do believe he was flirting with you," Betty said.

Mist smiled, remaining silent.

"He's a fine young man, one of my favorite guests." Betty continued. "He's spent many Christmases with us here."

"All the guests are wonderful," Mist said. She smiled as she added, "Even the professor, as long as he has his tea."

"Yes," Betty laughed. "He's quite a character. I found him grumbling outside this morning, saying the snow was already building up on the front walk right after Clive shoveled it."

Mist nodded. "There you have it, the dilemma and the solution. We can't control the snow, but we can control the tea. I believe that sums it all up." She checked the oven one more time, washed and dried her hands and left the kitchen.

CHAPTER ELEVEN

When Betty opened the doors to the café at 6 p.m., a long line of eager customers already waited, anticipating a Christmas Eve dinner unlike any that Timberton had experienced. Even William "Wild Bill" Guthrie himself was right up in front with Clayton and his fire crew. Others, not fond of lines or simply more patient, waited in the front parlor, where they enjoyed the hot mulled cider and baked Brie puffs that had been set out two hours before.

The hotel guests sat at their reserved table, having been given the courtesy of early seating. Their full plates didn't even make a dent in the spread that Mist had prepared. Laughter and high fives filled the air as townsfolk made their way along the buffet.

Mist was in high spirits herself, pleased to see the décor and cuisine had blended to create the festive atmosphere she'd desired. The scene matched the one on her sketchpad exactly. The sound of Bing Crosby's voice crooning Christmas songs from the café speakers rounded out the ambiance. The aromas from the holiday feast floated through the hotel like ribbons, tying everything together.

"Well. Look at this." Clive stood beside Mist, surveying the crowd. He'd passed up his usual first place in line for food in order to fetch more firewood. A long evening of camaraderie would undoubtedly follow the meal and the warmth of the fire would be welcomed.

"You look lovely." Clive had turned toward Mist, noting her appearance in a grandfatherly way. She'd taken a break in the late afternoon, once everything was under control. Casting aside her usual hippie chick gauze and batik clothing, she'd changed to a soft, red velvet dress that hung flapper-style around her slender figure. For shoes, she'd decorated a pair of ballet slippers with silver metallic paint, adding tiny swirls of red and white with a fine brush. A long string of pearls and a silver barrette with mother-of-pearl detail completed the outfit.

Mist smiled at the compliment. "I thought I'd get in the spirit of things."

"A mighty fine idea," Clive said. "In fact, a few people have been conspiring to allow you to enjoy this meal with everyone else." Mist raised her eyebrows in surprise as Clive guided her by the elbow to the table of hotel guests. An empty place waited for her, just to the right of Clara's and just to the left of Michael. She started to protest, but realized she was outnumbered. Resigned and slightly flustered, she sat.

"We all decided you've been working hard and deserve to enjoy the evening, too," Clara said, reaching over and clasping Mist's hand. "You know, many of us have been coming here for years, don't you, dear?"

"Yes," Mist said, her voice barely a whisper. "Betty told me. She looks forward to your visits each year as if you're family."

"Exactly how we feel about her, too," Clara said. "Even that old grump, Clive, seems like family now." The whole table laughed as Clara threw a teasing glance at Clive. Clive shook his head and headed off to grab a plate at the end of the buffet.

Michael leaned in Mist's direction. "You've made this year special for everyone here."

Mist turned her head toward Michael. "You're very kind, Michael. Betty and Clive have made this year special for me, too. It's been a great gift for me to be able to set up the Moonglow Café in this wonderful old hotel."

"Well, I'm quite chuffed to be here, if I do say so," Professor Hennessy said. "I was feeling a mite sorry for myself, being away from my family at this time of year. But the holiday spirit here is splendid." He paused. "And the tea is spot on! Just as delightful as my Aunt Margaret's tea back in London."

"Do you have Christmas in England?" Robert sat up straight in his chair as if he wanted the professor to treat his question like a serious, adult question.

"Yes, we do, young man," the professor said. "We have a splendid Christmas with a lovely dinner just like this. We always have plenty of roasted chestnuts, and on Christmas Day, we listen to the Queen's Christmas Message."

"That all sounds lovely, Professor," Ellen Greeley said. "You know, I feel like I'm the luckiest one of us. If not for Clive, I might still be stuck in that ditch."

Clive bowed at Ellen's praise, causing an awkward clunk as he placed a plate in front of Mist, whose eyes grew wide at the heaping portions of food, including both ham and roast. Not one spec of plate was visible; the meal threatened to spill over the sides, onto the table. "Clive! Thank you, but you know I can't eat all this!"

"What? Oh, sorry! Wrong plate!" Laughing, he switched it out with the plate in his other hand, one full of vegetables and absent of meat.

"Well, I'm lucky because I get to eat a chocolate tree tonight!" Robert bounced up and down in his chair.

"We're *all* looking forward to the chocolate tree, Mist," Sally said. "Robert told us all about it." Mr. Morrison nodded, waving a slice of kalamata olive bread in the air for emphasis.

Michael leaned toward Mist and lowered his voice. "Are we talking *Bûche de Noël*, aka Yule Log?"

"Yes, we are." It didn't surprise Mist that Michael caught on right away. He was unusual and endearing in many ways. She suspected she would miss him when he left.

Betty showed up at the table, removing plates from guests who had finished. Clara had to nudge Mist to keep her in her chair when she attempted to stand and help.

"You just relax, Mist," Betty said. "Marge and Maisie are helping clear dishes. Guests can help themselves to dessert on the side buffet. I already have coffee set up in the entry hall." She looked at the professor's raised eyebrows. "And tea," she added.

By the time the guests had moved into the living room and most townsfolk had gone home, Bing Crosby was done singing his entire repertoire of Christmas songs, and Nat King Cole had taken over. Clara and the professor had discovered a bowl of eggnog punch and were singing along to "Deck the Halls."

The Morrisons sat together, threading garlands of popcorn and cranberries for the tree. Robert handed over each popcorn kernel or cranberry as needed, a successful ploy to keep him from using a needle himself. Mist noticed all three were laughing together for the first time since they'd arrived.

Ellen Greeley stood by the front window, enchanted by the falling snow. Clive kept her company, pointing outside. Mist joined them for a moment.

"See that bench across the way? That's where Hollister sits in the spring taking it all in but never saying a word," Clive said.

"Who is Hollister?" Ellen asked.

"He's our mysterious, silent, homeless resident. We can't get him to come inside for more than a night or two."

"I'm hoping he comes in tonight, though," Mist said. "Even if he doesn't speak to anyone or see anyone, he has a spot in the back where the spirit of our festivities might reach him. And we always leave him food."

"That sounds like a lovely thing for you to do, Mist," Ellen said.

"It's not just me. The entire town takes care of Hollister."

"Well, I hope to meet him before I leave."

"Not likely," Clive said. "But he's an interesting one, Hollister. He may not use his voice, but sometimes he speaks volumes with his expressions and gestures."

"He sounds more expressive than my fiancé – er, ex-fiancé," Ellen said. "He was supposed to be here with me, but we called off the engagement. I nearly didn't come, but I'm so glad I did."

Mist placed a hand on Ellen's wrist. "We're delighted to have you here with us."

"That we are," Clive said. "His loss, if you ask me."

Mist left Clive and Ellen so that Clive could tell some of his taller tales of Timberton's past, recent and not-so-recent.

Mist saw that Michael sat near the tree, examining some of the older ornaments. "I'm especially fond of this one," he said, seeing Mist approach. He lifted a wooden star off the tree. "Carl Winslow made this a few years ago, whittled it right here by the tree. I watched him as he carved it."

"Clara's husband?" Mist connected the last name right away.

"Yes, this is her first year without him, which has been difficult. I think it gives her comfort, knowing the ornament is here. I've seen her stop by the tree to touch it now and then."

"Remembrances," Mist said.

"Yes, remembrances." Michael replaced the ornament on the tree.

"Exactly," Mist agreed. Conversation was so easy with Michael. Words were almost superfluous.

"It's a lovely tree this year," Betty said, stopping by with a pot of coffee in one hand. Maisie passed by right behind her, taking the coffee pot and heading off to refill cups.

"This is one of my favorites." Hands now free, Betty pointed to a miniature doll with a sweet bisque face. "This was my grandmother's. I just love old ornaments. They remind me of happy times in the past."

"How about new ornaments, to remind you of the future?" Clive had stepped up beside Betty and now reached around the tall tree. When he brought out the ornament he'd hidden behind the upper branches, Betty gasped with delight. The silver tree dangled from a narrow red ribbon, shiny metal and exquisite sapphire catching the white lights on the tree.

"It's beautiful, Clive!" Betty took the ornament in one hand, clearly touched that Clive had thought to craft it and hide it for a Christmas surprise.

"I thought I might start designing one each year. Build up a nice collection over time."

"Why, Clive, you could sell these in your gallery, along with the rest of the jewelry you design and Mist's paintings."

Clive grinned. "Well, now, I could, couldn't I? That's a darn good idea. But I'm not gonna do it."

"Why on earth not?" Betty asked. "This is beautiful. You know those late summer tourists we get in Timberton would buy them."

"Yes, I suppose they would. But I'm not making any for them. These are just for you." He put his arm around Betty, drawing her into a warm hug.

"That's a wonderful idea," Mist said. "You can look forward to this each year, something special in the future."

Michael smiled and nodded in agreement.

"Now, that's quite a statement, coming from someone who believes in living in the present," Clive said.

Mist smiled. "But the future *is* the present, Clive. It just hasn't happened yet." With that, she moved on, circling the room and noting the cheerful atmosphere. The professor had switched from the eggnog punch back to tea and was perusing the bookshelf. Clara and Sally Morrison sat together on the couch, deep in conversation. A sleepy Robert rested his head on his mother's lap. Ellen Greeley had just moved to the tree, admiring Betty's new ornament. Clive and Bob Morrison appeared to be heading back to the dessert buffet. A few townsfolk still lingered, knowing they were welcome to stay as long as they liked.

"A lovely evening, Mist." Michael had appeared by her side. He handed her a mug of hot mulled cider. "I've always loved spending Christmas here, but you've created something that is so special it's almost surreal. Look at everyone, content and peaceful."

"Just as it should be," Mist said. She took a sip of cider and leaned against the doorframe of the parlor. "Yes," she repeated, smiling. "Just as it should be."

CHAPTER TWELVE

Christmas morning arrived with bright sunshine. The storm, already lighter the day before, had disappeared completely, leaving a picturesque blanket of snow throughout the town. Even the tree branches sparkled in the morning light.

Mist had been up since before dawn, excited for Christmas Day. By 6 a.m., she'd brewed a favorite combination of French Roast and Hazelnut and set up coffee service in the silent hotel lobby while the guests slept soundly. Not even Robert had slipped down to sneak a peek at the presents below the tree. At least, not to her knowledge.

Maisie and Marge had done an amazing job cleaning up after the Christmas Eve feast. The front parlor and café stood ready for a new day. And the kitchen was spotless – a near-miracle after its heavy use the day before.

Mist filled muffin tins with cranberry-orange batter and placed them in the preheated ovens. She set a timer and returned to her room.

Seven miniature squares of canvas rested against the wall, their lower edges propped against her worktable. Looking across the assorted paintings, Mist knew she'd chosen images the guests would like. It had been just a whim when she'd first thought to do the paintings, something similar to a party favor. Now that she knew more about each guest, the gifts held more meaning. She was pleased that the guests would take home something tangible to remind them of their holiday at the Timberton Hotel.

When the timer buzzed, Mist returned to the kitchen to set the muffins out to cool. Back in her room, she wrapped each painting gently in rice paper, securing the thin paper with red raffia, and garnishing it with treasures from the box Maisie had given her. Tiny pinecones, paper berries and silk holly leaves added holiday cheer to the subtle wrapping. The gifts had no name tags, but she knew which went to each guest. She gathered them into her arms and passed through the front parlor on her way back to the kitchen, wedging each package between branches of the Christmas tree.

Mist found Betty in the kitchen setting out the ingredients Mist had requested for a Christmas Morning Scramble. "Everything in one pot," Clive had said, when he'd heard about the menu. Mist had laughed, revising his description to "Almost everything in one chafing dish." Still, his description had been fairly accurate. Aside from baskets of cranberry-orange muffins and a platter of fresh melon slices, breakfast would be one cheerful mixture of eggs, potatoes, cheese, mushrooms, sun dried tomatoes and fresh herbs. Small bowls of sautéed peppers and onions on the side would offer an option to spice the dish up.

Clara Winslow was the first to arrive, beating even Clayton and his crew. She wore a red sweatshirt with a puffy snowman design, black beads accenting the eyes and nose. Choosing just fruit and a muffin for breakfast, she moved into the front parlor, where Clive had just finished building a morning fire. The professor soon joined her to sit in the parlor with his morning cup of tea before moving into the café for a full breakfast.

Robert bounded down the stairs with the expected enthusiasm of a five year old on Christmas morning. His mother was right behind him. "Let's eat first, sweetie," she said, diverting him to the café before he ripped open the first present he could get his hands on. "You'll need energy before you tackle your gifts. And breakfast smells delicious."

"It does! It smells like magic food. Did Santa make it?"

"I don't think so. I think Mist did."

"Oh, same thing," Robert said. "She's magic, too."

One by one, the hotel guests and townsfolk passed through the café, offering Christmas greetings as they ate. Within an hour, most had gone off to enjoy a quiet day at home or a brisk walk or drive through the wintery countryside.

"I love that Christmas Morning Scramble, Mist," Sally Morrison said. "You must give me the recipe."

Mist had just stepped into the living room in time to see Robert tear into the first of several packages. "I'll be happy to. It's just a matter of herbs, really. You can change around the other ingredients according to your taste and whatever you have in your fridge."

Ellen Greeley sidled up to them. "Maybe you can add the 'scramble' recipe to the salad dressing recipe you promised me?"

"Of course!" Mist said.

"Merry Christmas, Mist!" Professor Hennessy toasted her with his cup of tea. He sported a Santa hat that looked both festive and odd next to his wire-rimmed glasses and mustache.

"A fire truck, cool!" Robert shouted, holding the shiny vehicle up in the air. He set it down immediately and started in on another present.

"We should see if Clayton would take him for a ride," Betty said.

Mist turned to see Betty had entered the room. "Excellent idea."

As the Morrisons exchanged presents, the single guests chatted with each other and delighted in witnessing Christmas through the eyes of a child. Clara surprised Betty with a box of caramels from Marge's store. These exchanges occurred to the music of much laughter and the backdrop of Christmas carols, some people sitting by the fire singing along. It was a cheerful and rowdy gathering.

Mist could hardly believe this was the same group of people who had arrived just days before, sadness trailing behind them. They'd managed to find hope in each other's company. Mist felt certain they would return to their own lives with powerful memories and encouragement that would help them all to move forward. Some would return as guests in the future, some would not. It wasn't something they could know now, just as Carl Winslow couldn't have known last year would be his last Christmas in Timberton. Whether these particular guests returned next year to spend the holiday together or not, Mist was certain they would never forget each other.

"I have something for each of you." The room quieted down at the unexpected sound of Mist's voice breaking into the merriment. She crossed the room, taking the first of the small packages from inside the tree.

"I'd like you to have this, Clara." She placed the wrapped painting in Clara's hands, smiling at the woman's surprised expression. This was the best part of giving an unexpected gift.

Clara looked around the room. "I certainly didn't expect this. You are too sweet."

"You don't need to open it now," Mist said, noting how shy Clara looked.

"Yes, she does!" Robert said. "I want to see!" Sally Morrison leaned forward to calm Robert down, but it wasn't necessary. Clara had already started to remove the festive wrapping. Her mouth formed an "O" when she unveiled the painting.

"It's lovely, Mist!" She turned the painting around for the other guests to see.

"What is it?" Robert wrinkled his nose.

"It's the quilt pattern from my room here," Clara explained. "See how it looks almost like a stained glass window?"

"What's stained glass?" Robert asked.

"It's the kind of glass you see in churches, dear boy. Oh, Mist, thank you so much. You know I adored that quilt the minute I saw it."

"This way you'll have it with you wherever you are."

Mist pulled another package out of the tree, sliding it cautiously past white twinkling lights. She took this one to the professor, who almost dropped his tea in surprise.

"For me?"

"Yes, for you," Mist reassured him.

"Well?" Robert again.

"Don't rush me, youngster," the professor said with mock seriousness. "It's not often I receive gifts from a stranger."

"No one's a stranger here," Mist said.

"Not for long, anyway," Betty said. "Once you walk in, you're family."

The professor shook his head as he pulled off the wrapping. "I never expected coming here would be like this. I expected to hide away and feel sorry for myself, being away from home at this time of year." He paused as he lifted up the painting. Smiling, he turned it around.

"That looks like your cup!" Robert was clearly pleased with himself. He'd won this portion of what now was a guessing game.

"Indeed it does," the professor agreed. "Quite remarkable! I'll hang this in my study when I get back to the university, right next to the chair where I always have my afternoon tea. You, my dear, remind me a little bit of my niece Katherine. Thank you."

Mist smiled as she pulled another package from the tree branches. She handed it to Ellen Greeley, who unwrapped the painting and turned it toward the group.

"It's a road," Robert said. "With a big sun above it."

"Yes," Mist said.

"Ah...for safe travels home," Michael said, watching as Mist nodded.

"A lovely idea," the professor agreed. "No running off into a ditch for you this time."

"Thank you, Mist," Ellen said. "I have a feeling this painting *will* bring me safe travels, both actual and personal. You seem to have a way with magic."

"Wow, you *are* a magician! I *knew* it!" Robert's face lit up in awe.

"Not at all," Mist laughed. "I just cook and paint. And listen to hearts."

"Like a doctor?" Robert's voice grew even more animated. "My doctor listens to my heart. He always listened to Joshua's heart extra 'specially closely because he said it had trouble beating right. I think that's why Joshua died, right Mommy, his broken heart?"

Mist glanced at Robert's mother to see if this question would send her back into her quiet grief. Her eyes did fill with tears, but she put her arm around her son and answered. "That's right, Bobby – I mean Robert. Joshua's heart got tired and that made him tired. But your heart is just fine." She kissed the top of Robert's head.

"That's what the doctor said! And he listened to it with this really cool metal steth...steth..." His arms gestured around his neck. "I'm going to be a doctor when I grow up. Like you, Miss Mist." Sally rubbed Robert's back.

Mist smiled. "I'm not a doctor, either, Robert. But I bet you'll be a great one."

"You don't have to be a doctor to listen to people's hearts," Michael added. He shifted his weight, adjusting the position of his leg, and then settled back in his chair.

The next package Mist pulled from the tree was for Michael. He paused before opening it. "Thank you." A brief second of eye contact passed between them before Robert spoke up.

"Open it. C'mon. I wanna see! What do you think it is?"

"I have no idea," Michael said, unwrapping the package. A slow smile crept across his face before he turned the painting around for the group to see.

"It's a rocking horse!" Robert clapped his hands.

"With a red scarf," Michael said. "A wonderful red scarf."

"Brilliant," the professor said. "The scarf practically glows. I believe there are specks of gold in it."

"Hey, what about us?" Robert said, hunching his shoulders and holding his arms to the side, palms up.

Mist looked up at the ceiling and tapped her chin, then looked back down at Robert. "Do you think I would forget you and your family?"

Robert's pouty look lasted only a few seconds before he smiled and shook his head. 'I don't think so...."

This time Mist pulled three packages from the tree, handing them all to Robert, whose eyes grew wide. "I get *three?*" A round of laughter circled the room.

"Oh, I get it!" Robert said. "One for each of us." He paused. "But how do I know which ones are for my mom and dad and which one is for me?" Everyone looked at Mist expectantly.

"It won't matter," Mist said.

"Because they're the same?"

"They are the same, and yet different," Mist explained.

Curious, Robert handed two of the packages out to his parents, then reevaluated and switched them around. Still deciding, he switched them again, finally satisfied he'd assigned them correctly. Sitting back down on the floor, he tore the wrapping off and held up his painting, just as others had done.

"Why, Robert," Clara exclaimed, "I believe that's the popcorn and cranberry chain you made last night." Others nodded in agreement, recognizing the round berries and puffs of popcorn.

"It's cool! It looks like a bumpy red and white snake!" Robert paused. "But it's just his body. His tail and head fell over the side." He turned the canvas sideways, seeing that the strand didn't continue over the edge. "No, they're missing. The popcorn snake lost its head and tail!"

"I'm not sure about that," Mist said. "Let's see what the others look like."

Robert turned to look at the other two paintings, which his parents now held up. The professor adjusted his glasses to get a better look.

"Mom got two popcorn snakes! And Dad's looks like mine, but sort of different." Robert turned his head from side to side, examining the paintings from different angles.

"Try putting them together," Michael suggested. Mist sent him a knowing smile.

Robert placed the three paintings on the floor, twisting them around like puzzle pieces. He tried several combinations, coming up with different designs every time. Finally he stopped at one particular combination. "Hey, it's one long snake without a head or a tail!" He looked at his parents and pointed at the design. "It's a circle! A circle snake!"

"A family circle," Clara whispered. "How lovely."

"They're all wonderful gifts, Mist," Clive said. He slipped his arm around Betty, who nodded in agreement. "And we have a little something for you," he added.

"Clive, Betty," Mist objected. "You are all my gifts. Time with you is enough. I don't need anything else."

Clive laughed. "I don't think you'll object to this. It's really for everyone." He stepped away from Betty and pulled a plastic bag out of his pocket, reaching inside. Lifting out a small cluster of leaves and berries, tied with a red satin ribbon.

"Mistletoe! I tried to get some earlier this week. I thought Maisie ran out." Mist looked at Betty, who appeared just as surprised.

"She did," Clive said. "All but one bunch, which she found this morning." He placed it on a hook above the archway to the parlor. "I thought I'd test it out." Before Betty could object, he pulled her over and planted a kiss on her forehead. Betty smacked him playfully with one hand and a round of applause followed. Clive laughed, "I knew that would work. Maisie was right. She said mistletoe had a way of bringing folks together."

"I get it!" Robert said. "Mist...Mistletoe...Get it? Get it?" The adults nodded in agreement.

"Well," Mist said, "how about some refills on Java Love and tea? And maybe more glazed cinnamon walnuts?" She eyed the empty dish on the table beside Michael's chair.

"A splendid idea," the professor said. "Especially the tea."

"I could go for more of those walnuts," Clara said, picking up the empty dish and following Mist to the kitchen.

Ellen Greeley stood and stretched. "I'm going to bundle up and take a walk. The weather is too beautiful to stay inside all day."

"I'll join you for a short one," Michael said, standing.

"I'll make sure the front walk is shoveled," Clive said.

"Snow play!" Robert jumped up, running for his coat, mittens and boots. "C'mon," he called to his parents.

In the kitchen, Mist filled the bowl for Clara, taking her up on an offer to serve the professor his tea, as well.

Finally alone with Betty, Mist refilled the hotelkeeper's coffee and made herself a cup of herbal tea. Looking around, they both saw the dishes that needed washing and knew they had an evening meal to prepare since all of the guests were staying one more night. They still had work to do.

As Mist set her mug of tea down and headed for the kitchen counter, Clive stuck his head in the side door.

"The Morrisons are building a snowman. Clara, Michael, Ellen and the professor have all offered to help. Are you ladies just going to work all day?"

Mist and Betty exchanged glances. Betty raised her eyebrows. Mist shrugged her shoulders.

"I think we can spare an hour," Betty said.

"Or two," Mist said, grinning.

"Well, then, get on out there!" Clive backed outside, laughing.

It was a rare day at the Timberton Hotel when Betty and Mist threw off their aprons and headed out simply to enjoy the day. But this wasn't just any day. Strangers had become family and chores could wait while they spent time with these people who had become dear.

As Mist followed Betty out the door, she looked back at the kitchen, taking in the stacks of dishes to be washed and ingredients to be prepped for dinner, all signs of camaraderie between guests. She smiled as she stepped outside and closed the door. No, this wasn't just any day. This was Christmas Day at the Timberton Hotel.

Betty's
Cookie Exchange
Recipes

Glazed Cinnamon Nuts
Cook's Nut Balls
Melting Moments
Ginger Crackle Cookies
Lemon Bars
Chocolate Chip Mint Cookies
Potato Chip Cookies
Chewy Coconut Cookies
Pumpkin Squares
Dark Chocolate Chunk Cookies
Yolanda's Chewy Oatmeal Raisin Cookies
Ricotta Cookies
Pecan Melts
Peanut Blossoms
Grandma's Shortbread Cookies
Holiday Eggnog Snickerdoodles
Spiced Apple Cookies
Almond Thumbprint Cookies
Salted Double Chocolate Chili Cookies
Oatmeal Chocolate Chip Cookies
Amish Ginger Cookies
Gluten Free Sugar Cookies
Mother's Sugar Cookies
Bourbon Balls

Glazed Cinnamon Nuts (a family recipe)

Ingredients:

1 cup sugar
1/4 cup water
1/8 teaspoon cream of tartar
Heaping teaspoon of cinnamon
1 tablespoon butter
1 1/2 cups walnut halves

Directions:

Boil sugar, water, cream of tartar and cinnamon to soft ball stage (236 degrees.)

Remove from heat.

Add butter and walnuts.

Stir until walnuts separate.

Place on wax paper to cool.

Cook's Nut Balls (a family recipe)

Ingredients:

1/2 cup butter
2 tablespoons sugar
1 cup flour
1 cup chopped nuts
1 teaspoon vanilla

Directions:

Mix all ingredients together and form into small balls.

Bake at 325 for 15-20 minutes.

Cool and roll in powdered sugar.

Makes about 18 cookies.

Melting Moments (submitted by Elisabeth Conley)

Ingredients:

1 cup brown sugar
1 cup butter
2 cups flour
Pinch of salt
1/2 teaspoon baking soda
1/2 teaspoon cream of tartar
3 teaspoons vanilla

Directions:

Cream together sugar and butter.

In separate bowl, sift together flour, salt, baking soda and cream of tartar; add to creamed mixture; add vanilla.

Drop on cookie sheet by teaspoonful.

Gently press flat with a fork dipped in milk.

Bake at 350 degrees until lightly browned, 10 minutes or less.

Ginger Crackle Cookies (submitted by Kim McMahan Davis, from her blog, *Cinnamon and Sugar and a Little Bit of Murder*)

Ingredients:

2 1/4 (10 ounce) cups flour
3 teaspoons ground ginger
1 teaspoon baking soda
1 teaspoon cinnamon
1/2 teaspoon ground cloves
1/4 teaspoon salt
8 tablespoons (4 ounces) unsalted butter at room temperature
1/4 cup (2 ounces) vegetable shortening
1 cup (8 ounces) granulated sugar, plus 2/3 cup for rolling
1 large egg
1/4 cup (2 fluid ounces) molasses
1/2 to 3/4 cup crystallized ginger pieces, finely chopped

Directions:

Position oven rack to the middle. Preheat oven to 350 degrees. Line cookie sheets with parchment or Silpat.

In large bowl, combine flour, ginger, baking soda, cinnamon, cloves and salt. Whisk until well blended.

In another large bowl, combine butter, shortening and 1 cup sugar. Beat with mixer on medium-high speed until well combined. Add egg and molasses and beat until well blended. Pour in the dry ingredients and mix on low speed until well blended. Add crystallized ginger and blend in.

Pour remaining 2/3 cup sugar into shallow bowl. Using a small scoop, make 1-inch balls with dough. Roll each ball in sugar and set 2 inches apart on cookie sheets. (If dough seems too soft to work with, place in refrigerator for a couple of hours.)

Bake one sheet at a time until puffed and slightly browned around the edges, about 10 - 13 minutes. Let cool on sheet for 5 minutes, then place cookies on wire rack to cool completely.

To make ahead:
The dough can be made, shaped and rolled in sugar through step 3, then frozen for up to 2 months before baking. For best results, position the shaped dough snugly on a small cookie sheet and freeze until very firm. Then pile the frozen balls into a heavy-duty freezer bag and store in the freezer. When you're ready to bake, remove only the number of cookies you need, place them on the prepared cookie sheet and leave them on the counter while the oven heats up. Bake as directed.

Lemon Bars (submitted by Carol Anderson)

Ingredients:

Crust:
1 cup butter
2 cups flour
1/2 cup powdered sugar

Lemon layer:
4 eggs
4 tablespoons flour
2/3 cup lemon juice
2 cups sugar

Directions:

Cream ingredients for crust together and pat into 9 x 12 pan. Bake at 350 for 15 minutes.

Mix ingredients for lemon layer together. Pour over baked crust.

Bake at 350 for 20 minutes.

Cool. Sprinkle with powdered sugar. Cut into squares.

Chocolate Chip Mint Cookies (submitted by Beth Britain, originally from Mollie Katzen's "Still Life with Menu")

Ingredients:

3/4 cup (1 1/2 sticks) butter

1/2 cup packed brown sugar

1/2 cup granulated sugar

1 egg

1 teaspoon vanilla extract

1 teaspoon peppermint extract

1 1/2 cups unbleached white flour

1/4 cup unsweetened cocoa

1 teaspoon baking soda

1/4 teaspoon salt

1 cup chocolate chips

Directions:

Preheat oven to 350 degrees.

Lightly grease a cookie sheet.

Cream together butter and sugars with an electric mixer at high speed. Beat in egg. Stir in vanilla and peppermint extracts.

Sift together dry ingredients and add them to the butter mixture along with the chocolate chips. Stir until well combined.

Drop by rounded teaspoons onto a lightly greased cookie sheet.

Bake at 350 for 12-15 minutes.

Remove from sheet immediately after baking and cool on a wire rack.

Potato Chip Cookies (submitted by Erika Bonham Kehlet)

Start with:

1 cup butter
1/2 cup sugar
1 teaspoon vanilla

Cream above ingredients together.

Add:

1/2 cup crushed potato chips
1/2 cup chopped pecans
2 cups flour

Roll into walnut sized balls.

Flatten with a glass dipped in granulated sugar.

Place on ungreased cookie sheet.

Bake at 350 degrees for 12-15 minutes.

Chewy Coconut Cookies (submitted by Valerie Peterson)

Ingredients:

2 cups sugar

1 cup shortening

2 eggs

1 teaspoon salt

1 teaspoon soda

1 teaspoon vanilla

2 cups flour

2 cups oatmeal

1 1/2 cups ground raisins

1/2 cup coconut

Directions:

Cream together sugar and shortening.

Add eggs, salt, soda and vanilla. Beat well.

Add flour, oatmeal and raisins. Add coconut last.

Roll in balls the size of a walnut.

Place on cookie sheet and bake at 375 degrees for 12 minutes.

Pumpkin Squares (submitted by Carol Ann Kauffman)

Crust:
1 cup flour
1/2 cup rolled oats
1/2 cup brown sugar
1/2 cup melted butter

Mix together. Spread on bottom of 9 x 13 pan. Bake 15 minutes at 350 degrees. Cool.

Filling:
1 pound can pumpkin
1 can evaporated milk
2 eggs
3/4 cup sugar
1/2 teaspoon salt
1/2 teaspoon cinnamon
1 teaspoon pumpkin pie spice
Pinch of nutmeg

Mix. Pour over crust. Bake 20 minutes at 350 degrees.

Topping:
3/4 cup walnut
1/2 cup brown sugar
2 tablespoons melted butter

Mix and spread on top of cooked pumpkin mix. Put back in oven for another 15 minutes.

Note: Double recipe for a cookie sheet size.

Dark Chocolate Chunk Cookies (submitted by S.A. Molteni, author of *I.T. Geek to Farm Girl Freak*)

Ingredients:

1 cup butter (2 sticks)
1/2 cup granulated sugar
1 cup packed brown sugar
1/2 teaspoon baking soda
1/2 teaspoon salt
2 eggs
1 1/2 teaspoons vanilla
2 1/2 cups all-purpose flour
1 giant Hershey's Dark Chocolate Bar chopped into chunks

Directions:

In a large mixing bowl, beat the butter with an electric mixer on medium to high speed for 30 seconds. Add brown sugar, granulated sugar, salt and baking soda. Beat mixture until combined. Add in the eggs and vanilla, beat until well blended. Beat in half of the flour, and then stir in remaining flour. Stir in chocolate pieces.

Drop dough by rounded teaspoons on an ungreased cookie sheet.

Bake at 350 degrees for 9-11 minutes or until edges are lightly browned.

Transfer cookies to a wire rack or wax paper and let cool.

Makes about 48 cookies.

Yolanda's Chewy Oatmeal Raisin Cookies
(submitted by Lisa Maliga, author of *The Aroma of Love*, from The Yolanda's Yummery Series, Book 3)

Ingredients:

1 cup unsalted butter, softened to room temperature

1 cup dark brown sugar

1/4 cup granulated sugar

2 large eggs (room temperature)

2 teaspoons vanilla extract

1 1/2 cups all-purpose flour

1 teaspoon baking soda

1 1/2 teaspoons ground cinnamon

1/2 teaspoon salt

3 cups rolled oats

1 1/2 cups raisins

1 cup chopped walnuts (optional)

Directions:

In a medium bowl, add the butter, brown sugar and white sugar. Mix on low to medium speed until creamy.

Add eggs and mix well. With a spatula, scrape the sides, and then add the vanilla extract. Mix well until combined.

In a larger bowl, mix the flour, baking soda, cinnamon and salt together. Add to the wet ingredients, and mix on low until combined.

Beat in the oats and raisins on low speed. Add the walnuts last.

For puffier cookies, refrigerate the dough for one hour.

Preheat oven to 350 degrees. Line two large baking sheets with parchment paper.

Using a standard tablespoon, scoop dough and place 2 inches apart on baking sheets. Bake for 10 minutes until lightly browned on the sides. The centers will look very soft and lighter in color.

Remove from the oven and let cool on baking sheet for 5 minutes before transferring to a wire rack to cool completely.

Ricotta Cookies (submitted by Lia Garret)

Ingredients:

2 cups all-purpose flour
1/2 teaspoon salt
1 tablespoon baking powder
1 cup sugar
1/2 cup butter, softened
1 8 ounce container ricotta cheese
1 teaspoon vanilla extract
1 large egg
1/4 to 1/2 teaspoon orange or lemon oil (optional)
Colored sprinkles (optional)

Directions:

Preheat oven to 350 degrees.

Mix flour, salt and baking powder together.

Cream butter and sugar together until light and fluffy.

Add ricotta, vanilla, egg and orange oil, mix well.

Stir in dry ingredients.

Drop by tablespoon on ungreased cookie sheet. If using sprinkles, add sprinkles before baking.

Bake about 15 minutes, until edges are very light brown.

Makes about 36 cookies.

Pecan Melts (submitted by Valerie Peterson)

Ingredients:

1/2 cup butter

1/3 cup sugar

1 egg (unbeaten)

1 cup flour

1/2 teaspoon salt

2 tablespoons orange juice

1/2 teaspoon grated orange rind

3/4 cup chopped pecans

Directions:

Cream together butter and sugar.

Blend in unbeaten egg.

Add half of the flour and salt.

Add orange juice and remaining flour and salt

Add grated orange rind. Stir in pecans.

Drop on cookie sheet by rounded teaspoons and bake at 350 degrees for 9-12 minutes.

Roll in powdered sugar while hot.

Peanut Blossoms (submitted by Carol Anderson)

Ingredients:

1 1/2 cups flour
1 teaspoon soda
1/2 teaspoon salt
1/2 cup sugar
1/2 cup brown sugar, packed
1/2 cup shortening or butter
1/2 cup smooth peanut butter
1 egg
2 tablespoons milk
1 teaspoon vanilla
Approx. 48 chocolate kisses (foil removed)
Additional granulated sugar for rolling

Directions:

Place all ingredients, except kisses, in a mixing bowl and stir until dough forms. Shape dough into balls about the size of walnuts. Roll balls in additional sugar and place on cookie sheet 2 inches apart.

Bake at 375 degrees for 10 minutes. Top each cookie immediately with a kiss. Press down firmly so cookie cracks around the edge.

Grandma's Shortbread Cookies (submitted by Debbie Brown)

Cook Time: 15 to 20 min.

Ingredients:

1/2 cup (125 ml) cornstarch
1/2 cup (125 ml) icing sugar
1 cup (250 ml) all-purpose flour
3/4 cup (175 ml) butter, softened

Directions:

Sift together cornstarch, sugar and flour. With wooden spoon, blend in butter until a soft, smooth dough forms.

Shape into 1-inch (2.5 cm) balls. If dough is too soft to handle, cover and chill for 30 to 60 minutes. Place 1 1/2 inches (4 cm) apart on ungreased baking sheets; flatten with lightly floured fork. Alternatively, roll dough to 1/4 inch (6 mm); cut into shapes with cookie cutters. Decorate with candied cherries, colored sprinkles or nuts, if desired.

Bake at 300 degrees (150 degrees C) for 15 to 20 minutes or until edges are lightly browned. Cool on wire rack.

To make crescents, add 1/2 cup (125 ml) ground almonds or hazelnuts to flour mixture. Shape into logs about 1/2 inch (1 cm) thick and 3 inches (7 cm) long. Curve into crescent shapes. When baked and cool, dip ends in melted chocolate.

Makes around 24 cookies.

Holiday Eggnog Snickerdoodles
(submitted by Diane Peterson)

<u>**Ingredients**</u>:

1/2 cup butter, softened
1/2 cup shortening
2 cups plus 1/3 cup sugar, divided
1 egg
1 teaspoon rum extract
1/2 cup evaporate milk
1/2 cup refrigerated French Vanilla nondairy creamer
5 1/2 cups all-purpose flour
1 teaspoon salt
1 teaspoon baking soda
1/2 teaspoon ground nutmeg

ICING:
1 cup powdered sugar
5-6 teaspoons French Vanilla creamer

<u>**Directions**</u>:

Preheat oven to 350 degrees. In large bowl, cream butter, shortening, and 2 cups sugar until light and fluffy. Beat in egg and extract.

In small bowl, mix milk and creamer.

In another bowl, whisk flour, salt and baking soda; gradually add to creamed mixture alternately with milk mix, beating well after each addition.

In a small bowl, mix nutmeg and remaining sugar. Shape dough into 1 inch balls; roll in nutmeg mix.

Place 2 inches apart on ungreased baking sheets; flatten slightly with bottom of glass.

Bake 10-12 minutes or until lightly browned. Cool on baking sheets for 2 minutes. Remove to wire racks, cool completely.

For icing: mix powdered sugar and creamer to reach desired consistency. Pipe snowflake designs on cookies.

Makes about 7 1/2 dozen cookies.

Spiced Apple Cookies (submitted by Valerie Peterson)

Ingredients:

1 cup raisins

1/2 cup shortening

1 1/3 cups packed brown sugar

1 egg

1/4 cup milk

2 1/4 cups all-purpose flour

1 teaspoon baking soda

1 teaspoon ground cinnamon

1/2 teaspoon salt

1/2 teaspoon cloves

1/2 teaspoon nutmeg

1 cup chopped walnuts

1 cup chopped unpeeled apple

Directions:

In small saucepan, cover raisins with water. Bring to boil, remove from heat. Cover and let stand for 5 minutes. Drain.

Meanwhile, in large mixing bowl, beat together shortening and brown sugar. Beat in egg and milk.

Stir together flour, soda, cinnamon, salt, cloves and nutmeg. Add to shortening mixture. Beat until well-blended.

Stir in nuts, apple and drained raisins.

Drop by rounded teaspoons on ungreased cookie sheet and bake at 375 degrees for 8 minutes. Immediately remove from cookie sheet and cool on wire rack.

Makes about 3 dozen medium cookies.

Almond Thumbprint Cookies (submitted by Debbie Brown)

Ingredients:

3/4 cup butter, softened

2/3 cup granulated sugar

2 eggs

1 1/4 cups ground almonds

2 cups baking flour

1/2 teaspoon ground cinnamon

1/2 teaspoon salt

1/2 cup apricot or peach jam

Directions:

Grease rimless baking sheets or line with parchment paper; set aside.

In a large bowl, beat butter with sugar until fluffy. Separate 1 of the eggs; drop white into a small shallow bowl and set aside. Add yolk and remaining egg to butter mixture; beat well.

In a separate bowl, whisk together 1/3 cup of the almonds, flour, cinnamon and salt; add to butter mixture in 2 additions and stir just until blended.

Lightly beat reserved egg white with 1 tablespoon water. Place remaining almonds in a shallow dish.

Roll dough by scant 1 tablespoon into balls. Dip each into egg white mixture; roll in almonds to coat. Place 2 inches apart on prepared pans. Using end of wooden spoon, make an indent in the center of each.

Bake in top and bottom thirds of 350 degree oven, rotating and switching pans halfway through until light golden, about 15 minutes. Press indent again. Transfer to wire rack; let cool. Fill indent with jam of choice. Or, before baking, press an unblanched almond into the cookie instead of making an indentation.

Makes about 35 cookies.

To make ahead: Layer between waxed paper in airtight container, and store for up to 2 days or freeze for up to 3 weeks.

Salted Double Chocolate Chili Cookies
(submitted by Kim McMahan Davis)

Ingredients:

1 1/3 cups all-purpose flour

2 tablespoons cornstarch

1 cup Dutch-processed cocoa powder

1 1/2 teaspoons flaky sea salt or kosher salt

3/4 teaspoon baking soda

3/4 teaspoon baking powder

1/2 to 1 teaspoon cayenne powder

3/4 cup unsalted butter, room temperature

1 cup packed brown sugar

3/4 cup granulated sugar

2 teaspoons pure vanilla extract

2 eggs, room temperature

1 1/2 cups semi-sweet or dark chocolate chips

Additional granulated sugar for rolling

Directions:

Preheat oven to 350 degrees.

Whisk the flour, cornstarch, cocoa powder, salt, baking soda, baking powder and cayenne powder together in a bowl. Set aside.

In a stand mixer fitted with the paddle attachment, cream butter until pale and fluffy, about 2 minutes, scraping down bowl as needed. Beat in sugars until smooth and fluffy again.

On low, add in vanilla and one egg at a time, scraping as needed, until incorporated.

Add in half the flour mixture on low and mix to incorporate before adding the other half.

Mix the flour in until just incorporated. Stir in the chocolate chips with a wooden spoon.

Refrigerate the dough for 12-24 hours, freeze the dough for about 1 hour, or bake the cookies straight away. There is less spread with chilled dough.

Roll the dough into tablespoon-sized balls and then roll in granulated sugar.

Place them about 2 inches apart on a parchment lined baking sheet.

Bake 10-12 minutes. Let cool briefly and then remove to a wire rack to finish cooling.

Makes about 32-40 cookies

Oatmeal Chocolate Chip Cookies
(submitted by Valerie Peterson)

Ingredients:

1 cup margarine
1 cup brown sugar
1 cup white sugar
2 eggs
2 cups flour
1 teaspoon baking soda
1/2 teaspoon salt
1/2 teaspoon baking powder
1 teaspoon vanilla
2 cups oatmeal
1 package chocolate chips

Directions:

Mix all ingredients in the order given.

Place by teaspoon on ungreased cookie sheet.

Bake at 350 degrees for about 10 minutes.

Amish Ginger Cookies (submitted by Debbie Brown)

Ingredients:

3/4 cup butter, softened
1 cup granulated sugar
1 egg
1/4 cup unsulfured molasses
2 1/2 cups all-purpose flour
1 teaspoon ground ginger
1 teaspoon ground cloves
1 teaspoon ground cinnamon
1 1/2 teaspoons baking soda
Additional granulated sugar for rolling

Directions:

Preheat oven to 350 degrees.

In a mixing bowl, beat together butter and 1 cup sugar until creamy. Add egg and molasses; beat until combined. Add the remaining ingredients and mix until well combined.

Roll dough into 1-inch balls and roll in the extra granulated sugar.

Place balls on ungreased baking sheet. Bake for 5 - 7 minutes until barely turning brown. Cool for 1 minute on baking sheet and then remove to wire racks to cool completely.

Makes about 48 cookies.

Gluten Free Sugar Cookies (submitted by Debbie Brown)

Ingredients:

1 1/2 cups white rice flour
1/2 teaspoon cream of tartar
1 1/2 teaspoons xanthan gum
1/2 teaspoon baking soda
1/8 teaspoon salt
1/2 cup butter or margarine
1 egg
1/2 teaspoon gluten free vanilla, lemon, or almond flavoring
1/2 cup sugar

Directions:

Preheat the oven to 350 degrees.

Mix the first 5 ingredients in a bowl. Once they are well combined, add the butter and mix together until ingredients become crumbly.

In a separate bowl combine the egg, flavoring and sugar and use a whisker to combine. Add this mixture to the dry ingredients. Mix it all until it recedes from the sides.

Shape the dough into a flat circle. Chill in the refrigerator for about an hour. Place the dough on freezer paper sprinkled with gluten free flour. You can substitute powdered sugar for the flour.

Roll out to 1/4 inch thickness, then cut with cookie cutters.

Place cookies on a lightly greased cookie sheet and bake for 12 minutes. Remove from oven when done and cool on wire rack.

Makes about 20 cookies.

Mother's Sugar Cookies (submitted by Barb Goss)

Ingredients:

6 cups flour

4 sticks margarine

2 cups sugar

4 eggs

4 teaspoons baking powder

2 teaspoons salt

1 cup milk

1 teaspoon vanilla

2 tablespoons anise seeds (or 3 tablespoons anise extract)

Directions:

Mix sugar, eggs and margarine.

Add milk.

Mix dry ingredients and combine gradually.

Roll out dough and cut with cookie cutters.

Bake at 350 degrees for 8-10 minutes.

*** Add more flour if necessary for firm batter.

*** Depending on egg size, you may need 7 cups of flour.

*** Thicker cut will be more cake-like, thinner cut will be crisper.

Bourbon Balls (submitted by Vicky Kaseorg)

Ingredients:

1 package vanilla wafers, roughly ground
1 cup chopped walnuts
3 tablespoons corn syrup
1/2 cup bourbon
Powdered sugar

Directions:

Put one bag of vanilla wafers in food processor until
roughly ground. Add walnuts.

Process into rice-sized pieces. Pour in bowl.

Add 3 tablespoons corn syrup.

Add 1/2 cup bourbon (or to taste.)

Roll in palms to form 1-inch balls.

Roll in powdered sugar.

Cover and chill or freeze up to one month.

ACKNOWLEDGEMENTS

A Christmas novella sounded like a cheerful holiday treat, and so Mistletoe at Moonglow came to be. As with longer stories, it took a village the size of fictional Timberton to pull this tale together. Developmental support and several magical spells of editing came from the always awesome Elizabeth Christy. Credit goes to Keri Knutson of Alchemy Book Covers for cover design, as well as to Leah Banicki and Tim Renfrow for formatting eBook and print editions. Sincere thanks go out to Chef Marc Boussarie for giving Mist a few inspirational culinary tips, and to Carol Anderson for her proofreading expertise. And Jay Garner and Paul Sterrett deserve cheers of gratitude for being patient with me while I bounced ever-changing ideas around their brains.

It also didn't seem fair that only Betty's guests at the Timberton Hotel would enjoy a festive cookie exchange. So when you tie that apron on and start mixing ingredients, send a nod of appreciation to the wonderful readers and authors who submitted recipes: Carol Anderson, Beth Britain, Debbie Brown, Elisabeth Conley, Kim McMahan Davis, Lia Garet, Vicky Kaseorg, Carol Ann Kauffman, Erika Bonham Kehlet, Lisa Maliga, S.A. Molteni, Diane Peterson and Valerie Peterson.

Recipe Notes

Recipe Notes

Recipe Notes